Heartstrings on the Horizon

Riverbend Valley Book 3

Tara Baisden

STERLING RIDGE PRESS LLC

Cover designed by Sterling Ridge Press LLC

Published by: Sterling Ridge Press, LLC www.sterlingridgepress.com

ISBN: 978-1-966093-13-8
Printed in the United States of America

First Edition: April 2025

For permissions, contact: tara@tarabaisden.com or visit www.tarabaisden.com

About The Author

Tara Baisden is a Contemporary Christian Inspirational Romance author who proudly calls the beautiful state of West Virginia her home. Nestled on a sprawling mountainous property, she is surrounded by the peace and serenity of nature. Her days are happily spent in the quiet of country life, writing heartwarming stories of love, faith, and second chances. Tara also enjoys quilting, working in her garden, tending to her beloved pets, and soaking in the beauty of her surroundings.

With deep roots in West Virginia, family is everything to Tara. One of her favorite pastimes is gathering on the front porch with loved ones, sharing stories, laughter, and enjoying the simple, meaningful moments that life offers. When she's not crafting her novels, Tara can often be found exploring the rich history of her home state, visiting local historical sites, and, of course, stopping by every bookstore she passes! Her passion for reading and discovery always fuels her next adventure.

Tara is the author of the Laurel Ridges series of novels, as well as the Riverbend Valley series of novels, of which have been beloved by fans of inspirational romance. Her novels reflect her love for faith, family, and the timeless beauty of the world we live in.

Known for her sweet and clean romances, she creates characters that feel like family and settings that make readers want to visit again and again.

You can find out more about Tara and her latest releases at www .tarabaisden.com or follow her on social media for updates and behind-the-scenes glimpses of her writing process. Stay connected—you won't want to miss the heartfelt stories of love and family she has in store!

Also by Tara Baisden

<u>Riverbend Valley Series</u>

#1 A Cowboy's Second Chance

#2 Wanderlust & Wild Horses

#3 Heartstrings on the Horizon

<u>Laurel Ridge Series</u>

#1. Season of Hope

#2. Finding Grace

#3. His Perfect Plan

#4. Love Redeemed

#5 Snowbound Blessings

#6 Sheltered Hearts

#7 Restoring Faith

#8 Love Rekindled

#9 Where She Belongs

#10 Shelter in His Arms

#11 Where Love Stands

About Riverbend Valley

Welcome to the fictional town of Riverbend Valley, Montana!

Nestled in the shadow of the breathtaking Sapphire Mountains, Riverbend Valley is a place where life flows as peacefully as the rivers winding through it. Surrounded by rolling ranch lands, dense forests, and the rugged peaks of Montana's wilderness, this picturesque valley is the perfect setting for tales of faith, love, and second chances.

A Rugged Heritage

Founded in the late 1800s by homesteaders drawn to the fertile land and expansive views, Riverbend Valley began as a ranching settlement. Riverbend Valley's roots run deep, forged by generations of ranchers and cowboys who've worked the land with grit and determination. This is a place where faith has always been a cornerstone, guiding its people through hardships and celebrating their triumphs. From the well-worn pews of Riverbend Valley Community Church to the lively gatherings at the rodeo grounds, Riverbend Valley's traditions reflect a steadfast commitment to God, family, and the land.

A Community of Faith

Riverbend Valley offers a refuge for weary souls and a chance to rediscover the beauty of life's simple pleasures. Whether it's through a quiet moment of prayer along the river, a moonlit ride under Montana skies, or the laughter of a community united in celebration, this is a place where hearts are mended, faith is renewed, and love abounds.

The Essence of Small-Town Life

With a population of just over three thousand, Riverbend Valley retains its small-town charm. Main Street is lined with family-owned businesses, from the Bluebird Café, famous for its huckleberry pies, to the General Mercantile, where locals gather to swap stories and stock up on supplies. Seasonal festivals bring the community together, from the Spring Rodeo to the Fall Harvest Festival, celebrating the rhythms of life in this ranching town.

A Haven for Visitors

Visitors to Riverbend Valley are captivated by its rustic charm and natural beauty. Whether it's horseback riding through the foothills, fishing in the Deer Run River, or stargazing from Silver Bluff's iconic overlook, there's something for everyone to enjoy.

Experience the Heart of Riverbend Valley

Here, under the endless skies and among the resilient people of Montana, you'll find stories of redemption, second chances, and unwavering faith. Riverbend Valley isn't just a setting—it's a celebration of the rugged heritage and timeless grace that make this place unforgettable. **Welcome to Riverbend Valley, where faith is strong, family is everything, and love always finds a way.**
I hope you fall in love with its enduring spirit.

Dedication

To all the dreamers brave enough to leave the familiar behind and chase what their hearts know to be true.

To the writers who dare to tell the stories burning in their souls, even when it means taking the road less traveled.

And especially to every person who has ever felt out of place, searching for where they truly belong. May you find your own Silver Bluff Ranch—that special place where your heart feels at home and God's purpose for your life becomes crystal clear.

"For I know the plans I have for you," declares the LORD, "plans to prosper you and not to harm you, plans to give you hope and a future." - Jeremiah 29:11

And to all my readers - may you find the courage to embrace your own authentic journey, wherever it may lead.

With gratitude and hope,

Tara

Contents

Chapter 1

Emma Carlyle stared at the blinking cursor on her laptop screen, a digital taunt mocking her creative paralysis. The sleek, minimalist decor of her Los Angeles apartment, usually a source of calm, now felt sterile, reflecting the emptiness echoing within her. Sunlight streamed through the panoramic windows, showcasing the city's glittering skyline, but the vibrant energy of LA buzzing outside her window felt muffled, distant, as if she were viewing it through a thick wall of smoke.

A framed book cover on the built-in shelving unit caught her eye. *Accidentally Ever After*. Crimson lettering against a backdrop of a ridiculously handsome couple laughing in Paris, France. *Bestseller*, the gold foil lettering, proudly proclaimed. It felt like a relic from another life, a testament to a success that now tasted like ash in her mouth.

Emma pushed back from her desk, the ergonomic chair sighing in protest. She wandered over to the floor-to-ceiling windows, her gaze drifting over the cityscape.

Ten months.

Ten months since Liam had knelt—not in a loving proposal as she'd foolishly believed—but to confess. Confess not just to having cold feet, but a cold heart. His words, polished and rehearsed as any Hollywood script, still echoed with icy clarity. "It's not you, Emma, it's me. I'm just not... wired for this kind of commitment." Wired. Like he was some kind of faulty appliance, easily returned to sender.

She traced a condensation trail on the cool glass with a fingertip; the city blurring into indistinct blobs of color. It was her, though, wasn't it? Something about her wasn't right, wasn't enough. Successful author, yes. Bestselling, even. But apparently, not... lovable. Not wife material. The rom-com queen couldn't even script her own happy ending.

The relentless pressure of churning out happily-ever-afters, deadline after deadline, had felt invigorating once, fueled by ambition and the thrill of seeing her words resonate with readers. Now, it just felt... hollow. Each perfectly constructed meet-cute, every witty banter exchange, each inevitable grand gesture of love felt like another nail hammered into the coffin of her own romantic ideals.

Her current novel, ironically titled *Cowboys & Confetti*, sat mocking her in its digital file. Cowboys. Confetti. She'd pitched it to her publisher, Preston House Publishing, months ago, riding the wave of her previous successes. "Cowboy romance is hot right now, Emma! Give us your signature sparkle, but with spurs!" her agent, Brenda, had chirped enthusiastically. Sparkle. Right. Emma felt about as sparkly as week-old dishwater.

She wandered back to the desk, her fingers hovering over the keyboard. Blank. The screen remained stubbornly, infuriatingly blank. No witty opening lines for the next chapter danced in her mind. No charming characters clamored for attention. Just... static. Mental and emotional static.

Emma clicked away from the dreaded document and mindlessly scrolled through the internet, a digital wanderer seeking... she wasn't even sure what. Distraction? Inspiration? A sign?

Then, a headline snagged her attention: *Escape to Montana: Silver Bluff Ranch Offers an Authentic Cowboy Experience.*

Montana. Cowboy. The words jumped out, a sudden jolt in the monotonous scroll. She clicked. The webpage opened, flooding her screen with images that were a stark contrast to the steel and glass of her urban existence. Rolling plains stretched under vast, impossibly blue skies. Horses grazed in sun-drenched pastures, their coats gleaming. Rugged mountain ranges framed the horizon, their peaks dusted with snow even in early summer. And then there were the cowboys, silhouetted against a fiery sunset, their hats casting long shadows as they worked horses in a corral.

Emma scrolled through the article, her finger instinctively dragging the mouse down, down, captivated by the descriptions of Silver Bluff Ranch. Family owned, the article proclaimed, steeped in generations of Montana ranching tradition. Grace Walker, the ranch owner's daughter, ran a dude ranch on the property, inviting people to come and experience real ranch life. Horseback riding, lessons in horsemanship, cozy tiny homes, home-cooked meals, and evenings spent under a canopy of stars, listening to stories around a crackling campfire.

Campfire.

Stars.

Real cowboys.

The words resonated, stirring something deep within her. It was the opposite of everything Los Angeles, everything her suffocating rom-com world represented.

Authentic.

Real.

Grounded.

An image flashed across the screen—a tiny home, nestled among pine trees, a porch swing gently swaying in the breeze. Silver Bluff Dude Ranch offered tiny home accommodations, the article high-lighted. Charming, rustic, and comfortable. Perfect for immersing oneself in the ranch experience.

Immersion.

That word resonated, too. Immersion was undoubtedly what she needed. If she was going to write cowboy romance, really write it, not just churn out another formulaic story, she needed to experience it. She needed to breathe the air, smell the leather and hay, feel the grit of the Montana dust. She needed to understand the heart of a cowboy, not just the chiseled jaw and Stetson hat.

And maybe, just maybe, a change of scenery, a break from the relentless city hum, was precisely what her soul needed too. A chance to breathe again, to find a flicker of her lost spark in the vastness of the Montana landscape.

Before logic could catch up, Emma clicked the "Book Now" but-ton. Dude Ranch Experience. Silver Bluff Ranch. Riverbend Valley, Montana. Dates flashed across the screen. Availability. Tiny Homes. Activities. Prices.

Her fingers danced across the keyboard, filling in the fields. Dates—next week. Escape Los Angeles. Escape her apartment. Escape the blank screen and the suffocating expectations. Escape Liam's ghost and the ghost of her own broken heart. Tiny Home—why not? Go all in. Four week stay. Activities—all of them. Horseback riding—even though her riding experience was limited to a pony ride at a childhood birthday party. Learn ranch operations—she had no idea what that even entailed, but curiosity bubbled up, a tiny effervescent whisper in the stagnant pool of her burnout.

Confirmation. Payment processed. Email received. It was done. She was going to Montana. To a dude ranch for four weeks. To learn about cowboys and write cowboy romance, and rediscover herself in the rugged beauty of the West.

A nervous flutter tickled her stomach, a mix of excitement and trepidation. Montana was... Montana. Vast. Wild. Completely outside her comfort zone of perfectly manicured LA life. She pictured herself, city-slick Emma Carlyle, stumbling around a ranch, completely clueless, probably covered in dirt. The image was both shocking and oddly appealing.

She chuckled, a small, rusty sound that felt unfamiliar in the quiet apartment. Maybe a little dirt was exactly what she needed. To ground her, to remind her of the real world beyond book deadlines and publishing pressures and broken engagements.

Emma leaned back in her chair, a sense of lightness blooming in her chest. It was impulsive, reckless even, this Montana adventure. But for the first time in months, she felt a flicker of genuine excitement, a spark of hope igniting in the ashes of her burnout.

She opened her laptop again, this time not to the blank document, but to her blog. *City Girl Goes Cowboy*. The title popped into her head, a playful promise of the adventure to come. Her fingers flew across the keyboard, words tumbling out, not forced or contrived, but flowing with a newfound ease. She wrote about her burnout, her broken engagement, her desperate need for a change. She wrote about discovering Silver Bluff Ranch and the impulsive decision to book a stay. She wrote about her hopes, her fears, her plan to become a cowboy romance author.

As she typed, she could almost feel the Montana air on her face, smell the scent of pine and horses. The blank screen had been replaced with a canvas of possibility, a vast, untamed landscape waiting to be explored. And for the first time in a long time, Emma Carlyle felt ready to paint her own story, not just write about someone else's.

She ended her blog post with a promise to her readers, her loyal followers who had been with her through every rom-com release, every book signing, every online chat. She promised to share her Montana adventure, the triumphs and the inevitable blunders, the beauty and the grit, the cowboys and the... maybe not confetti, but definitely the wide-open spaces and the possibility of something new. She hit publish, a surge of adrenaline coursing through her veins. Then she shared it on her social media channels. The Los Angeles fade-out had begun. Montana, and Silver Bluff Ranch, awaited.

Chapter 2

The rental car, a cherry-red sedan that felt ridiculously out of place amidst the rugged landscape, bumped along the gravel road. Dust billowed behind it like a cinnamon cloud. Los Angeles, with its smog-tinged sunsets and concrete landscape, was receding further and further with each mile she drove, replaced by an unfolding panorama that stole her breath.

Emma gripped the steering wheel, knuckles white, not from tension, but from a strange mix of exhilaration and awe. The interstate had given way to a two-lane highway, then a county road, and now this bumpy gravel lane—a track carved through a tapestry of sagebrush and wildflowers. The air, crisp and clean, rushed in through the open windows, carrying scents—pine needles warmed by the sun, the sweet tang of drying grass, and something else, something earthy and animalistic, the faint but unmistakable aroma of horses.

The Sapphire Mountains. The name had sounded romantic in the online article, almost too good to be true. Now, as they rose majestically in the distance, their snow-dusted peaks piercing the impossibly blue sky... romantic felt like an understatement. They were raw, powerful, ancient. These weren't the manicured hills of Southern California, but something altogether different, something wild and untamed that resonated deep in Emma's soul.

She rounded a bend, and the gravel crunched louder under the tires. A wooden sign appeared on her right: **Silver Bluff Ranch — Welcome**. Further down the road, a sign with an arrow pointed down a narrower drive directing her toward the Silver Bluff Dude Ranch, flanked by a split-rail fence that stretched as far as the eye could see. Horses, dark shapes against the lush grasses, dotted the vast pastures beyond the fence. Real horses. Not the carousel ponies of her childhood memories, but powerful, graceful creatures, heads lowered, grazing in serene contentment.

A thrill, sharp and unexpected, shot through Emma. This was it. No more city noise, no more deadlines looming, no more ghosts of broken promises. Just open sky, wide-open spaces, and... cowboys. The thought brought a nervous flutter to her stomach, a mix of anticipation and sheer cluelessness. What had she gotten herself into?

As she drove further down the lane, the ranch buildings began to emerge from the landscape. Not sprawling mansions or glitzy resorts, but sturdy, functional structures built of wood and stone, blending seamlessly with the natural surroundings. A main lodge, its wrap-around porch adorned with rocking chairs, stood at the heart of the ranch, flanked by barns, corrals, and what looked like a riding arena. Tiny homes, nestled among stands of pine trees, were scattered along the periphery, hinting at the 'rustic-chic' accommodations she'd booked.

Emma slowed the car, her senses overwhelmed. The sounds—the chirping of unseen birds, the distant lowing of cattle, the rhythmic swish of a horse's tail. The air, so different from the recycled, air-conditioned air of her apartment, filled her lungs with invigorating freshness. The vastness of the sky, the sheer scale of the landscape, made her feel simultaneously small and strangely liberated.

She pulled up in front of the main lodge and parked, switching off the engine. The silence that descended was profound, broken only by the gentle creaking of the porch swings in the breeze and the rustle of leaves. For a moment, Emma simply sat, absorbing the quiet, letting the Montana air wash over her. It was a balm to her frazzled nerves, a tangible shift from the frenetic energy of her city life to a rhythm that felt slower, more deliberate, and somehow... right.

Taking a deep breath, she opened the car door and stepped out. Her city-slicker sandals felt incongruous on the gravel, a jarring reminder of her outsider status. She straightened her sundress, smoothed down her radiant blonde hair, and reminded herself to appear confident, or at least not completely lost. This was research, after all. Immersion. She was here to learn, to observe, to soak it all in. And maybe, just maybe, to heal a little.

The front door of the lodge swung open, and a woman stepped out onto the porch. Sunlight framed her silhouette, but even from a distance, Emma could sense a warmth radiating from her. She was tall and slender, with a welcoming smile that reached her kind eyes. A silver cross necklace glinted at her throat, catching the sunlight.

"Emma?" the woman called out, her voice clear and friendly, carrying across the distance. "Welcome to Silver Bluff Ranch! I'm Grace."

Relief flooded Emma. A real, genuine welcome. Not the practiced robotic smiles of Los Angeles, but something authentic, something that felt like it came from the heart. She walked towards the porch, a hesitant smile blossoming on her face.

"Grace? It's so good to finally be here," Emma replied, her voice sounding a little breathless, even to her own ears. "Thank you for having me."

Grace descended the porch steps and extended a hand, her grip firm and warm. "We're thrilled to have you, Emma. I know you've come a long way. Come on in. Let's get you settled."

As Emma followed Grace into the lodge, she took in her surroundings. The interior was just as inviting as the exterior, with exposed wooden beams, a stone fireplace dominating one wall, and comfortable leather sofas and armchairs scattered around the room. The scent of lemon furniture polish and something baking—cinnamon rolls, maybe? — filled the air. It felt less like a hotel lobby and more like stepping into someone's home. A warm, welcoming home.

"Let me take your bag," Grace offered, gesturing towards the suitcase Emma had pulled from her back seat. "And then we can get you checked in and show you to your tiny home."

"Thank you," Emma said, handing over the suitcase. "Everything is just... beautiful. Pictures really don't do it justice. I feel like I'm in another world that I may never want to leave!"

Grace chuckled, a warm, genuine sound. "Montana has a way of doing that. It gets under your skin, you know? Changes you." She led Emma to a rustic wooden counter that served as the reception desk. "We're a bit more laid-back here than your average city hotel, but we like to think we offer a different kind of luxury. The luxury of space, of peace, and real connection."

"I already feel at peace," Emma admitted, leaning on the counter. "It's... quiet. In the best possible way. And lovely!"

"Peace and quiet for the soul," Grace agreed, her eyes twinkling. "That's what we aim for here at Silver Bluff. A place where people can reconnect with themselves, with nature, and with what really matters in life."

Grace efficiently checked Emma in, explaining the ranch's schedule, mealtimes, and the activities available. As she spoke, Emma noticed a small, worn Bible lying open on the counter beside a guest registration book. It wasn't prominently displayed, not preachy, but its presence spoke volumes about the values that underpinned Silver Bluff Ranch.

"Your tiny home is 'Bluebird'," Grace said, handing Emma a key attached to a carved wooden bird. "It's just a short walk from the lodge, nestled against the woods. I think you'll love it. It's got everything you need—a comfy bed, a small kitchenette, a private porch with a swing. And a view that'll knock your socks off."

"It sounds perfect," Emma said, her excitement growing.

"Let me show you the way," Grace offered, leading Emma through a back door and out onto a winding path that led to several tiny homes. The path was lined with wildflowers, splashes of vibrant color against the green undergrowth.

As they walked, Grace chatted easily, asking Emma about her journey, her impressions of Montana, and her plans for her stay. Emma relaxed in Grace's company, her initial nervousness melting away in the face of her genuine warmth and easygoing nature.

"So, Emma," Grace said casually, as they rounded a bend and a charming blue tiny home came into view. "Are you by any chance... the Emma Carlyle?"

Emma blinked, surprised. "The... author Emma Carlyle? Yes," she said, a little self-consciously. "Is that... a problem?"

"I knew it!" Grace laughed, a delighted sound. "Problem? Hardly! I'm a huge fan! My book club devoured 'Accidentally Ever After' last year. We absolutely loved it. And 'Meet Me in Manhattan' was just pure sunshine on a page. I am thrilled about hosting a celebrity author here at Silver Bluff!"

Emma flushed, pleased but slightly embarrassed by the unexpected praise. "Oh, wow, thank you. That's... really kind of you to say."

"Kind? It's the truth! You have a real gift, Emma. That sparkle, that wit, that way of making characters come alive... it's magic." Grace stopped in front of a tiny home, gesturing for Emma to precede her up the steps to the porch.

"Well," Emma began hesitantly, "that's actually... part of why I'm here." She stepped onto the porch, admiring the charming swing and the breathtaking view of the mountains that unfolded beyond. Grace followed her, unlocking the door to the tiny home.

"Oh, this is adorable!" Emma exclaimed, stepping inside. The tiny home was indeed charming, with rustic wood walls, cozy furnishings, and large windows that let in the natural light. It was compact but thoughtfully designed, with a comfortable-looking bed, a small kitchenette tucked into one corner, and a compact but modern bathroom. It felt both cozy and airy, rustic yet comfortable.

Grace set Emma's suitcase inside the door. "Make yourself at home. Since it's so late in the day, you'll find plenty of options if you're hungry in the fridge and an assortment of snacks in your pantry cupboard. I'll leave you to unpack and settle in. A tour of the ranch starts in about an hour. We'll meet at the lodge. Casual dress. And Emma?"

"Yes?" Emma asked, sensing a shift in the conversation.

"You said you were here... partly because of your writing?" Grace prompted gently.

Emma hesitated for a moment, then took a deep breath. This felt like a safe space, a place where she could be honest, vulnerable, without the judgment or expectations of her city life. "Yes," she confessed. "Well, kind of. I mean, I am an author, as you know. A rom-com author. But... things have been a little rough lately. Burnout, broken engagement... my life just started feeling... hollow."

Grace nodded, her expression understanding. "I get it. Sometimes we all need to escape the noise and find our way back to ourselves."

"Exactly," Emma agreed, relieved that Grace seemed to understand. "And... well, I'm at a crossroads in my career, too. My contract with my publisher is up, and... I'm not sure if I want to keep writing rom-coms."

"So, what do you want to write?" Grace asked, her eyes full of genuine curiosity.

Emma took another deep breath, this time feeling a surge of excitement bubbling up within her. "Cowboy romance," she declared, the words feeling both audacious and liberating as they left her lips. "Western cowboy romance and self-publish them on my own. That's... that's the dream."

Grace's eyebrows rose in surprise, then a wide smile spread across her face. "Cowboy romance? Seriously? Emma Carlyle, queen of rom-coms, writing cowboys?"

Emma laughed, feeling the tension ease further. "I know, right? Sounds crazy. I've wanted to write those kinds of books for a couple of years now. Something just clicked when I saw the article about Silver Bluff Ranch. Montana cowboys... it felt like a sign. Like this was where I needed to be. To learn, to experience, to... immerse myself in the real cowboy life so I can write about it authentically."

"Authentically," Grace repeated, thoughtfully. "I like that. And you think Silver Bluff Ranch can help you with that?"

"I hope so," Emma said earnestly. "I mean, I know I'm here for the whole dude ranch experience, and a vacation, but... I'm really serious about this. I want to understand it, the lifestyle, the values, the... heart of it all. I intend to write cowboys who feel real, not just like cardboard cutouts."

Grace was silent for a moment, her gaze thoughtful. Then she smiled again, a slow, genuine smile that lit up her face. "Emma," she said, her voice warm and encouraging, "I think you've come to the right place. And I think... I think we can do more than just give you the 'dude ranch experience'."

Emma's heart leaped with anticipation. "Really? What do you mean?"

"Well," Grace said, stepping back onto the porch, gesturing to the vast ranch beyond the tiny home. "Silver Bluff Ranch is more than just a dude ranch. It's a working ranch. My brother, Garrett, runs the quarter horse operation. It's been in our family for generations. Real Montana ranching, real cowboy life. And... I think, if you're serious about wanting to learn, I think we can give you a hands-on glimpse behind the scenes. A taste of the real West."

Emma's eyes widened, hope surging through her. "You mean... you'd let me?"

"Let you?" Grace chuckled. "Honey, I'd be delighted. I've always loved books. And I admire someone who's brave enough to chase a new dream, to step outside their comfort zone. And besides," she winked, "it'll be fun to see a city girl try her hand at ranch life."

Emma laughed, relief and gratitude flooding her. "I'm warning you, I'm completely clueless. My ranch experience is limited to watching old westerns on television and eating steak."

"Don't worry," Grace reassured her, clapping her on the shoulder. "We'll start you slow. Maybe begin with mucking stalls. Always a glamorous ranch job." She grinned mischievously. "But seriously, Emma, I'm happy to take you under my wing. Show you the ropes. Introduce you to the real cowboys of Silver Bluff. Including my brother, Garrett."

As Grace mentioned her brother's name, something flickered in her eyes, a subtle undercurrent of something Emma couldn't quite decipher. Intrigue? Mischief? Or something else entirely?

A sound drifted on the breeze—the rhythmic thud of hooves, the creak of leather, the low murmur of voices. Emma turned, following the sound, and saw them. Riders emerging from behind a stand of trees, silhouetted against the vast expanse of the pasture. Cowboys. Real cowboys. Moving with a natural grace and confidence that was both captivating and slightly intimidating.

In the lead, riding a magnificent black quarter horse, was a figure that drew Emma's eye immediately. He was broad-shouldered, with a Stetson pulled low over his brow, casting his face in shadow. Even from this distance, she could sense an aura of ruggedness, of quiet strength, that radiated from him. He moved with the horse as if they were one, an effortless partnership born of long hours in the saddle, of a deep connection to the land and the animals.

He reined in his horse near a corral, dismounting with a fluid motion. He moved with an economy of effort, every gesture purposeful, every movement reflecting a deep familiarity with the ranch and its demands. He spoke to the other riders, his voice low and resonant, too distant to hear the words, but carrying a note of authority, of command. Then, he turned his back to the tiny homes, facing towards the horses in the corral, and began to work, his movements focused, intent. Oblivious, it seemed, to the presence of the dude ranch guests, to Emma, to everything beyond the horses and the task at hand.

Emma watched him for a moment longer, a strange mix of curiosity and nervousness swirling within her. He was... undeniably compelling. Ruggedly handsome, in a way that was both raw and refined.

"That's Garrett," Grace said, her voice breaking through Emma's reverie. "My brother." There was a note of wry affection in her voice.

Emma turned back to Grace, pulling her gaze away from Garrett. "He's... very... ranchy," she said, feeling a little foolish for the cliché, but unable to find a more articulate description.

Grace laughed again. "Ranchy? That's one word for it. Stubborn, dedicated, loyal, and... maybe a little brooding. He's been through a lot." There was a shadow of sadness in her eyes.

Emma sensed a story there. "What do you mean?" she asked, her curiosity piqued.

Grace hesitated for a moment. "It's a long story. One for another time, maybe. But just... be patient with him, Emma. He's got a good heart, underneath it all. A very good heart. And a lot of faith. This ranch, this family, it's all built on faith, you know? Faith in God, faith in each other, faith in the land. It's what gets us through the tough times."

"Faith," Emma repeated, the word resonating in the quiet Montana air.

"Well," Grace said, clapping her hands together, breaking the moment. "Enough about brooding cowboys and ranch philosophy. I'll leave you to unpack and get settled? Then, join me back in the lodge in about an hour. I'll be giving a tour of the ranch. Show you the horses, the barns, the whole shebang."

"That would be wonderful," Emma said. "Thank you, Grace. For everything."

"My pleasure, Emma," she said. "Welcome to Montana. Welcome to Silver Bluff Ranch. Welcome to the real West." She turned and walked back down the path, leaving Emma alone, surrounded by the beauty of the Montana landscape.

Emma stepped back inside, closing the door behind her. She leaned against the door for a moment, taking another deep breath, letting the Montana air fill her lungs. *Welcome to Montana. Welcome to the real West.* The words echoed in her mind, carrying a promise, a challenge, and a whisper of something new.

She turned, surveying her cozy, tiny home, a sense of contentment settling over her. It wasn't the luxurious apartment she had left behind in Los Angeles, but it was perfect. Simple and comfortable. It was a sanctuary, a place to breathe, to think, to write, to... rediscover herself.

She unpacked her suitcase, hung clothes in the small closet, and arranged her toiletries in the bathroom. As she unpacked her laptop, instead of the familiar wave of dread, a flicker of anticipation sparked within her. Here in Montana, surrounded by real cowboys and the vast, untamed landscape, she could finally find the inspiration to breathe life into those horrible, lifeless chapters she'd attempted before. Write a story that is more than just sparkle and wit and perfect characters. Write something with heart, something with depth, something... real.

She set the laptop aside, deciding to leave the writing for later. For now, she was eager to explore, to soak it all in, to experience the ranch, to meet the people, to breathe the Montana air.

Chapter 3

Ranch tour.

The words spun in Emma's mind. She was actually doing this. Ditching the stilettos for... well, she wasn't quite sure what ranch tour footwear entailed, but her sneakers would have to suffice for now.

She smoothed a hand over the denim sundress she'd chosen, an attempt to look somewhat ranch-appropriate. Maybe it was too cliché? A city girl in denim trying to fit in. This whole trip was about stepping outside her comfort zone, and that included ditching the carefully curated image she projected in LA.

A quick check in the small bathroom mirror... blonde hair slightly windblown already, a touch of color in her cheeks she hadn't seen in months, and a definite spark of anticipation in her eyes. The Montana air was already working its magic.

Taking one last look around the tiny home, ensuring she had her phone and a small notebook tucked into her purse, Emma stepped out onto the porch. The swing swayed gently in the breeze, an invitation to relax, to slow down. But not yet. Ranch tour first.

She followed the winding path back toward the main lodge; the gravel crunching under her sneakers. The surrounding sounds seemed amplified, the distant whinny of a horse, the rhythmic clang of metal from the direction of the barns, the cheerful chirping of meadowlarks perched on fence posts. It was a symphony of rural life. A comforting rhythm with a sense of peace woven into the sounds.

As she approached the lodge, she spotted Grace on the porch, chatting with a couple who looked like they were in their late fifties, dressed in matching plaid shirts and brand-new cowboy hats. Dude ranch guests, Emma surmised.

Grace waved as she saw Emma approaching, her smile warm and welcoming. "Emma, perfect timing! Come and meet Carol and Tim. They're here from Arizona and ready to fully immerse themselves in the ranch life as well."

"Hi Emma," Carol said, her voice friendly, though Emma detected a hint of polite curiosity in her eyes, a subtle sizing-up. Tim nodded a hello.

"It's so nice to meet you both," Emma replied, offering a genuine smile. She was consciously trying to project warmth, to be open and approachable, shedding the guardedness she sometimes wore as a shield in LA.

"Emma is a writer," Grace announced with a flourish. "A very successful one, actually. She's here to experience the ranch lifestyle and write about it." Grace's wink was subtle, but Emma caught it, a silent encouragement.

Carol's eyes widened slightly. "Oh, really? What kind of books do you write?"

"Rom-coms, mostly," Emma explained. "But I'm working on something new. Cowboy romance."

Tim chuckled, a deep, rumbling sound. "Cowboy romance, huh? Well, you've come to the right place for inspiration." He gestured around the ranch with a sweep of his hand. "Plenty of cowboys around here."

Carol smiled, more genuinely this time. "That sounds lovely. I love a good romance. Maybe you can put Silver Bluff Ranch in your books!"

"Maybe I will," Emma said.

Grace clapped her hands together. "Alright, let's get this tour started! Everyone ready to see the heart of Silver Bluff?"

"Born ready," Tim declared, adjusting his hat. Carol nodded enthusiastically.

"Excellent! Emma, come on, or if you'd rather explore on your own..." Grace offered, giving her an out.

"No, I'll go with you," Emma said.

"Perfect! Let's start with the heart of the dude ranch—the arena," Grace announced, leading the way off the porch and towards a large, red structure slightly set apart from the main ranch buildings.

As they walked, Grace pointed out various features of the ranch, her voice filled with a quiet pride. "The dude ranch is on the south side of the property," she explained. "My brother, Garrett, manages the quarter horse operation on the north side. It's a separate business, though we all work together, of course. The dude ranch helps keep the whole place afloat, especially these days. Ranching isn't always easy, nor profitable at times." There was a subtle shift in her tone, a hint of the real-life challenges behind the idyllic ranch facade.

The scent of horses grew stronger as they approached the arena, a rich, earthy aroma mixed with the sweet smell of hay. The sounds shifted too. The soft nickering of horses, the rhythmic rustling of hay, and the occasional stamp of a hoof.

Grace swung open the heavy wooden doors, and Emma stepped inside, her senses immediately overwhelmed in the best possible way. It was a symphony of equine life. Rows of stalls lined the edges of the arena, each occupied by a magnificent horse, their coats gleaming in the dappled sunlight that streamed through the high windows. The air was warm and still.

"This is where the magic happens. Meet the stars of Silver Bluff Dude Ranch." Grace said with a smile.

Emma walked slowly down the aisle around the outer edge of the building, gazing into each stall, mesmerized by the beauty and quiet power of the horses. They were various colors and breeds, each with its own unique personality reflected in its eyes and stance. Some were calmly munching hay, others were watching her with curious gazes, and a few let out soft, welcoming nickers.

Tim and Carol were equally captivated, their faces alight with childlike wonder. Carol reached out a tentative hand to stroke the velvety nose of a chestnut mare, who nudged her gently. Tim was already peppering Grace with questions about breeds, training, and ranch history.

Grace answered him patiently, her knowledge of horses and ranch life evident in every word. She introduced them to several horses by name, sharing snippets of their personalities and histories.

As they reached the end of the aisle, Grace stopped in front of a stall occupied by a striking black gelding with intelligent, dark eyes. "And this is Diablo," she said, her voice softening slightly. "He's one of our most experienced trail horses. And quite a character."

Diablo watched them with a regal air, his head held high. There was something about him, a quiet intensity, that drew Emma's attention.

"He's magnificent," Emma breathed, drawn to Diablo's presence.

"He is," Grace agreed, nodding. "He's one of my brother's personal horses, actually. Garrett uses him for some advanced trail rides... when he has time. Garrett has a special connection with Diablo."

Garrett. The name echoed in Emma's mind. The brooding cowboy in the pasture from earlier. She wondered if Diablo's quiet intensity was a reflection of his owner.

A figure emerged from the shadows at the far end of the barn, walking towards them with a purposeful stride. His presence filled the space, radiating strength and an undeniable magnetism.

He was dressed in worn jeans, a denim shirt with the sleeves rolled up to reveal strong forearms, and scuffed cowboy boots that spoke of countless hours spent in the saddle and on the ranch grounds. His Stetson was pushed back slightly on his head, revealing a glimpse of dark brown hair and a face that was even more ruggedly handsome up close than she had imagined. His eyes, a deep, intense blue, scanned the group, pausing briefly on Emma, a flicker of... something unreadable in their depths before shifting to Grace.

"Grace, I need you to sign off on the vet's bill for..."

"Garrett, perfect timing!" Grace exclaimed, her voice bright. "Tim, Carol, this is my brother, Garrett Walker." She turned to Emma, "And Garrett, this is Emma Carlyle. She's our guest also, and a bestselling author. She's here to... experience real ranch life."

"Tim, Carol... nice to meet you and welcome."

Garrett's blue eyes turned to Emma again, this time lingering a moment longer, assessing. His expression remained neutral, reserved, but there was a flicker of curiosity.

"Ms. Carlyle," he said, his voice deep and resonant, with a subtle Montana drawl that sent a shiver down Emma's spine. "Welcome to Silver Bluff." His tone was polite and formal. He offered a curt nod, but no handshake.

"Mr. Walker," Emma replied. "It's... a pleasure to meet you."

Pleasure? Perhaps not exactly the right word.

Intriguing? Definitely.

Intimidating? A little.

Captivating? Undeniably.

"Garrett runs the quarter horse operation here," Grace continued, smoothly bridging the slight awkwardness. "He knows everything there is to know about horses and ranching. He's the real deal." She beamed at her brother, but Garrett's expression remained unchanged, a hint of a frown deepening the lines around his eyes.

"Grace," he said, his voice a low rumble, "the vet bill." It was a gentle reminder, a subtle push to get back to ranch business. He was polite, but clearly not interested in small talk.

"Right, right," Grace said, a little flustered. "Sorry. Emma, Tim, Carol, why don't you take a few minutes to admire the horses? Garrett and I just need to... discuss a few things." She subtly steered Garrett away from the group, towards a tack room at the back of the arena.

Emma watched them go, a strange mix of disappointment and intrigue swirling within her. He was definitely... something. Ruggedly handsome, yes, but it was more than that. A definite air of... sadness? Or perhaps just weariness.

"Well, he's certainly... a cowboy," Carol murmured, breaking the silence, her tone a little breathy.

Emma turned back to the horses, trying to refocus her attention, to shake off the unexpected impact of Garrett's brief appearance. Diablo was still watching her, his dark eyes intelligent and knowing. She reached out a hand and stroked his soft muzzle. He nuzzled her hand in response, a warm, gentle touch.

"He likes you," a soft voice said from behind her.

Emma turned, startled. Standing nearby was a little girl, her eyes wide and bright, her blonde hair braided neatly, a splash of freckles dusting her nose. She couldn't be more than five or six years old. She was dressed in jeans and a t-shirt with a horse on it.

"Oh, hello," Emma said, smiling at the girl. "He does, doesn't he?" She stroked Diablo again. "He's beautiful."

"He's the best," the little girl declared with absolute certainty. "He's my daddy's horse."

"Your daddy?" Emma asked, her gaze instinctively drifting towards the tack room where Garrett and Grace had disappeared.

The little girl nodded solemnly. "Garrett's my daddy."

"I'm Emma," she said.

Ellie's face lit up, her shyness melting away instantly. "Emma? The book lady?" Her eyes were wide with wonder.

Emma blinked, surprised again. "Yes. How did you know?"

"Aunt Grace told me," Ellie said matter-of-factly. "Are you going to write a cowboy book?" she asked, her voice full of innocent curiosity.

"I'm hoping to," Emma replied. "That's why I'm here. To learn about cowboys and ranches, so I can write a really good story."

"Cowboys are cool," Ellie declared, puffing out her chest slightly. "My daddy is the best cowboy ever."

"I'm sure he is," Emma agreed, glancing again towards the tack room. Garrett and Grace were still inside, their voices muffled.

"Do you want to see the kittens?" Ellie asked suddenly, her attention already shifting to a new adventure. "Really fluffy ones!"

"Kittens sound wonderful," Emma said, smiling at Ellie. "Lead the way."

Ellie grabbed Emma's hand, her small fingers surprisingly strong, and led her towards a pile of hay in the corner of the arena. Tim and

Carol were still admiring the horses, engrossed in their own ranch experience, oblivious to Emma's detour.

Tucked into a cozy nest of hay were a cluster of tiny kittens, their eyes barely open, mewing softly. Their mother, a sleek calico cat, watched them with vigilant eyes, purring contentedly.

"Oh, they are adorable!" Emma breathed, her heart melting at the sight of the tiny, fluffy creatures.

Ellie beamed, settling down beside the kittens, gently stroking one with a delicate finger. "This one is Patches," she announced. "And this one is Stripey. And this one is... I haven't named her yet." She looked at Emma, her eyes wide and pleading. "Can you help me name her?"

Emma's heart warmed. "I would love to help you name her," she said, settling down beside Ellie in the hay. "Let's see... what does she look like?"

The kitten was a tiny ball of white fluff, with one tiny black spot on her ear. She mewed softly, reaching out a tentative paw towards Emma.

"She's like a little angel," Emma murmured, stroking the kitten gently. "Maybe... Angel would be a good name?"

Ellie considered it, her brow furrowed in thought. "Angel... hmm. Maybe. Or... Snowflake?"

"Snowflake is pretty too," Emma agreed. "Or... how about... Montana?"

Ellie's eyes widened. "Montana? Like... Montana the kitten?" She tested the name, her voice soft. "Montana... I like that. Montana the kitten." She beamed, her face alight with happiness. "Thank you, Emma!"

"You're welcome, Ellie," Emma said, smiling. "It's a perfect name."

The sound of a firm, masculine voice calling Ellie's name broke the spell.

"Ellie? Where are you, peanut?"

"Daddy! Over here!" Ellie said, holding up the kitten proudly. "We named her Montana! Do you like it?"

"Ms. Carlyle," he said, his tone formal again.

"We were just admiring the kittens," Emma explained, keeping her tone light and friendly.

Garrett's gaze lingered on Emma for a moment longer, his blue eyes searching hers, unreadable.

He reached out and gently stroked the kitten, a hint of a smile tugging at the corner of his lips. "Montana, huh? That's a good name."

Ellie beamed, snuggling Montana closer. "Emma named her! She's a really good namer, Daddy."

Garrett's gaze shifted back to Emma.

"Is that so, Ms. Carlyle?" he asked, a subtle teasing note entering his voice. "You're good with kittens and names?"

Emma's heart fluttered again. "I suppose I am," she replied, meeting his gaze, a small smile playing on her lips.

Chapter 4

Emma hesitated on the wide front porch of the lodge, taking in the early morning activity through the open windows. Laughter and conversation drifted out, accompanied by the clinking of plates and silverware. The aroma of fresh coffee and bacon made her stomach rumble.

She smoothed her hands over her jeans and adjusted the plaid button-down shirt she'd bought specifically for this trip. The outfit felt foreign, like she was playing dress-up.

Taking a deep breath, Emma pushed open the heavy wooden door. Warmth and light spilled out, along with a wave of delicious breakfast smells—coffee, bacon, something sweet and cinnamony. The large dining room to the right bustled with morning energy as ranch hands and guests gathered around a massive farmhouse table.

Grace spotted her immediately. "Emma! Come in, come in! You're just in time." She waved Emma over to an empty chair between herself and Ellie, who bounced excitedly in her seat.

"Emma!" Ellie beamed. "Mama Linda made cinnamon rolls. They're the bestest ever."

A woman with silver-streaked dark hair tied back in a neat bun emerged from the kitchen, carrying a steaming platter. Her eyes crinkled warmly as she set it down. "Mornin'! I'm Linda Ross, ranch cook and self-appointed mother hen to this whole bunch. Sit yourself down, honey. Coffee?"

"Coffee would be wonderful, thank you," Emma replied, settling into the chair between Grace and Ellie. The seat offered a perfect view of the entire dining room, and what a view it was.

The farmhouse table dominated the space, crafted from rich, dark wood that spoke of history and family gatherings. Morning light filtered through the large windows, illuminating the room's rustic elegance.

A distinguished-looking man in his sixties sat at the head of the table, his weathered face creased with laugh lines despite his current serious expression as he studied what appeared to be ranch paperwork. His arthritic hands moved slowly but deliberately as he made notes.

"Daddy," Grace said, touching the man's arm. "Put the paperwork away. Emma, our guest, joined us for breakfast."

He looked up, his eyes warm and gentle. "So she has." He set the papers aside. "Judd Walker. Welcome to our table, Emma."

"Thank you, Mr. Walker."

"Just Judd, please. Mr. Walker makes me feel older than I already am." He chuckled, a rich, warm sound.

Another woman emerged from the kitchen, her silver-blonde hair swept into an elegant twist, carrying a basket of warm biscuits. "Oh! You must be the writer Grace mentioned." Her smile lit up her entire face. "I'm Loretta, Judd's better half and mother to these two." She gestured to Grace and Garrett, who had just walked in from outside, his boots leaving dusty prints on the hardwood floor.

"Garrett Walker," she scolded good-naturedly, "what have I said about filthy ranch boots in my house?"

Garrett paused, looking down at his boots with a hint of chagrin. "Sorry, Mama." He turned, stepping back onto the porch to remove them.

"Daddy always forgets," Ellie stage-whispered to Emma, giggling behind her hand. "Grandma says he'd forget his head if it weren't screwed on."

Emma bit back a smile as Garrett returned. He slid into the chair next to Ellie, who immediately leaned against him.

Three more people filed in from outside—a tall man with graying hair who moved with quiet confidence, a younger man whose eager energy practically radiated off him, and a woman with dark hair pulled back in a practical braid, all of them in ranch style work clothes.

"Raven, Clint, Wyatt—come meet one of our guests," Grace called out. "This is Emma Carlyle."

"The writer?" The younger man—Clint—asked, his face lighting up with interest as he dropped into a chair. "Grace mentioned you. I read that article about you in California Living magazine last month!"

Emma blinked in surprise. "You read California Living?"

"Only when I'm desperate in the feed store waiting room," he admitted with a grin.

"Clint reads anything that isn't nailed down," the woman—Raven—said, settling into her chair. "I'm Raven Thompson. Don't mind him, he's just excited to meet someone famous."

"I wouldn't say famous," Emma demurred.

"Bestselling author counts as famous in these parts," the older man said. "Wyatt Mason. I've been working at Silver Bluff Ranch longer than some of these youngsters have been alive."

Linda placed a steaming mug of coffee in front of Emma, the rich aroma mingling with the breakfast scents filling the room. "Cream and sugar are on the table, dear. Help yourself."

Tim and Carol entered just then, looking slightly uncertain in their matching plaid shirts. Grace waved them to empty seats across from Emma. "Perfect timing! Now we're all here. This is Carol and Tim everyone, they are from Arizona."

Nods and greetings were shared as Loretta began passing platters of food—golden biscuits, crispy bacon, fluffy scrambled eggs, and the promised cinnamon rolls that had Ellie practically vibrating with anticipation.

"Grace mentioned you're writing a book about cowboys," Raven said, accepting a platter from Wyatt. "That must be quite a change from your usual books."

Emma nodded, carefully selecting a biscuit. "It is. But sometimes change is precisely what a person needs."

"That's the truth," Judd agreed, his voice thoughtful. "Change brought us all here to the lodge to live as a family, didn't it, Loretta?"

"The lodge?" Emma asked, her curiosity piqued.

Grace nodded. "The main lodge was originally built just for the dude ranch guests, about four years ago. But then..."

"The fire," Loretta finished. "One night, just a few months after we finished the lodge, an electrical fire started in the walls of our ranch house."

"Lost everything," Judd added as he patted Loretta's hand. "But the Lord works in mysterious ways. We had this beautiful new lodge sitting here, plenty of space. So instead of rebuilding..."

"We expanded," Grace explained. "Added private family quarters, made the kitchen bigger to accommodate both guest meals and family life. Turned what was meant to be just a dude ranch lodge into a real home."

"Best decision we ever made," Linda said, returning with a fresh pot of coffee. "Having everyone under one roof—it's like the old days, when families really lived and worked together."

"Except when someone's practicing their roping in the living room," Loretta said pointedly, looking at Clint.

The young ranch hand had the grace to blush. "That was one time, Mrs. Walker. And I paid for that vase."

"You sure did," Wyatt chuckled. "Three months of extra mucking duty, as I recall."

"So, all the employees live here as well?" Emma asked.

"Well, we are all employees here on the ranch in one way or another. All of us Walkers live here in the lodge. The ranch hands, Wyatt, Raven, and Clint, live in the bunkhouse, so they are a bit closer to where they work. We're all just one big happy family here at Silver Bluff," Loretta said.

"Do you live in the lodge, too?" Emma asked Linda, buttering a warm biscuit.

"I do," Linda nodded, finally settling into her own chair. "Have my own little suite upstairs. I've been cooking for the Walkers going on fifteen years now. When the old house burned..." She paused, her eyes growing distant. "Well, they didn't even hesitate to include space for me here. That's the kind of folks they are."

"She's family," Loretta said simply. "Has been since the day she showed up with a pie and offered to help when I was laid up with a broken ankle."

"Bringing that pie sealed the deal," Linda said, her eyes twinkling.

"Emma, you should see Linda's cookbook collection. She's got recipes handed down through generations of ranch cooks," Grace said.

"Really?" Emma leaned forward, her writer's curiosity piqued. "Traditional ranch recipes?"

"Some dating back to the 1800s," Linda confirmed. "Course, I've modified them over the years. Can't imagine cooking on a wood stove like my great-grandmother did."

"Daddy says the old recipes are the best ones," Ellie piped up, carefully spreading jam on her biscuit. "He says they put hair on your chest!"

A surprised laugh escaped Emma as Garrett nearly choked on his coffee.

"Ellie," he said, clearing his throat, "I don't think that's exactly what I said."

"But you did say Miss Linda's cooking could bring a dead man back to life," Ellie insisted. "Remember? When Mr. Peterson was sick and—"

"More eggs, anyone?" Linda interrupted smoothly, though her eyes danced with amusement.

The conversation flowed naturally around the table, weaving between ranch business, local gossip, and gentle teasing. Emma found herself drawn into the warmth of it, the easy familiarity these people shared. Even Tim and Carol seemed to relax into the welcoming atmosphere.

"Speaking of recipes," Grace said, passing the cinnamon rolls, "Emma, you should try one of these. They're Linda's specialty."

"And a closely guarded secret," Judd added, his weathered face creasing with amusement. "Even Loretta doesn't have this recipe."

"A woman needs her mysteries sometimes," Linda said primly, though her eyes twinkled.

Emma selected a cinnamon roll, the sweet aroma making her mouth water. As she took a bite, warm flavors of cinnamon, butter, and something she couldn't quite identify melted on her tongue.

"Oh, my goodness," she murmured. "This is incredible."

"Told you!" Ellie said triumphantly. "Mama Linda makes the bestest breakfast ever. And lunch. And dinner. And sometimes she makes special treats just for me when I help feed the chickens."

"You help with the chickens?" Emma asked, genuinely interested.

"Uh-huh. Daddy says I'm the prettiest egg collector in Montana." Ellie sat up straighter, pride evident on her small face. "Want to come see them after breakfast? I can show you where the chickens hide their eggs."

Before Emma could respond, Garrett cleared his throat. "Ellie, remember what we talked about? Ms. Carlyle is here as a guest. She probably has plans with Aunt Grace today."

"Actually," Grace interjected, "I thought Emma might like to see some real ranch work today. Maybe even give it a try herself. If you're interested, Emma?"

Emma nodded eagerly. "That's exactly why I'm here. To learn, to understand."

"Well then," Judd said, setting down his coffee cup, "might as well start with the basics. Grace, why don't you show her the ropes? And I mean that literally." He chuckled at his own joke.

"Well," Raven said, reaching for another biscuit, "if you're going to learn ranch work, you'll need proper boots. Those sneakers won't last a day in the barn."

Emma felt her cheeks warm. "I did pack boots. They're just... new. And stiff."

"New boots are like new horses," Wyatt said sagely. "Take some breaking in before they're worth anything."

"Speaking of horses," Grace said, "we should get Emma started with the basics today. Mucking stalls, feeding, grooming. Build up to riding."

Garrett, who had been quietly focused on his breakfast, looked up. "Make sure she starts with Sugar. That old mare's got more patience than a saint."

"Sugar's my favorite," Ellie announced. "She lets me brush her tail and everything. Maybe I could help teach Emma?" She looked hopeful between her father and aunt.

Garrett's expression softened as he looked at his daughter. "Tell you what, peanut. You help Mama Linda with the breakfast dishes like you promised, then maybe you can go out to the barn later after you collect the eggs. Deal?"

"Deal!" Ellie beamed. "Emma, you'll love Sugar. She's brown and white and has a star on her face, and she loves carrots and—"

"Breathe, sweetheart," Loretta said fondly. "Let Emma eat her breakfast."

Tim leaned forward, clearly interested. "What about us? Carol and I signed up for riding lessons."

"You'll be with my mom this morning," Grace assured them. "She'll start you with the basics—grooming, tacking up, learning to read a horse's body language."

"Body language?" Carol asked nervously.

"Horses talk plenty," Wyatt explained. "Just not with words. You learn to read their ears, their eyes, the way they hold themselves. It's like..." he paused, considering, "like reading a book, but one written in a different language."

Emma perked up at the analogy. "That's fascinating. Subtle communication, and unspoken language."

"You sound like a writer," Raven observed with a slight smile.

"Always," Emma admitted. "Everything's potential material."

"Lord help us," Clint laughed. "We're all going to end up in a book."

"With names changed to protect the guilty," Linda added, beginning to clear empty plates.

"Here, let me help," Emma offered, starting to rise.

"Sit," Linda ordered firmly. "You're a guest. Besides, Ellie and I have a deal, don't we, sugar?"

Ellie nodded solemnly. "Yep! I'm the best dish dryer in Montana, too."

The morning sun strengthened, casting long shadows through the dining-room windows as breakfast wound down.

"Best get moving," Wyatt announced, rising from his chair. "Those fence posts in the north pasture won't fix themselves."

Clint jumped up eagerly. "I'll get the tools loaded in the truck."

"I'll head to the barn, start the morning feed. Grace, want me to get Sugar ready for Emma?" Raven asked.

"That would be great, thanks," Grace nodded. "We'll be out shortly."

Ellie had already bounded to the kitchen, her small voice drifting back as she chattered to Linda about proper dish-drying technique. The sound of running water and clinking plates created a homey background noise.

"Lord willing, it'll be a good day for ranch work," Judd said, easing himself up from his chair. His movements were careful and deliberate, a testament to years of hard physical labor. "Grace, make sure Emma here starts slow. Ranch work has a way of using muscles that city folks don't know they have."

Emma smiled, thinking of her regular yoga sessions back in LA. Somehow, she suspected a downward dog hadn't prepared her for what lay ahead.

"Don't worry, Daddy," Grace assured him. "We'll take it easy."

Loretta began gathering the remaining plates, her movements efficient and practiced. "Emma, honey, if you're going to be working in the barn today, you might want to pull your hair back. I have extra hair ties if you need one."

"That's kind of you, thank you," Emma replied, suddenly conscious of her perfectly styled waves. Another remnant of city life that would need adjusting.

Garrett stood, his chair scraping softly against the floor. "I've got that meeting with the horse broker in town," he reminded Grace. "Shouldn't take me too long."

"Daddy, can I come?" Ellie called from the kitchen, hope evident in her voice.

"Not today, Ellie," he called back. "Remember? You promised to help Linda with the chickens after dishes."

A small sigh drifted from the kitchen, followed by Linda's gentle murmur of encouragement and the clink of another plate being washed.

Tim and Carol looked slightly overwhelmed by the flurry of morning activity. "Should we change clothes before the riding lesson?" Carol asked, plucking at her crisp new shirt.

"Those'll do fine," Grace assured her. "Though you might want to grab a hat. The Montana sun can be fierce, even in the morning."

Emma watched the easy flow of conversation and movement around her, the natural rhythm of a household well-versed in their morning routine. It was so different from her solitary breakfast routine in LA—a protein smoothie grabbed between email checks and phone calls.

Garrett opened the front door and stepped out onto the porch to pull his boots. Emma couldn't help noticing how the morning light caught a little silver threading through his dark hair at the temples, softening his features.

"Grace," he said, looking up. "Don't forget, we need to discuss the fall booking schedule later. And Emma—" He hesitated, seeming to choose his words carefully. "Watch Sugar's left side when you're grooming. She favors it."

Emma nodded, oddly touched by this small piece of practical advice. "I will. Thank you."

He put on his Stetson and tipped it slightly—a gesture so quintessentially cowboy that Emma had to suppress a smile—and headed out.

"Well," Grace said, pushing back her chair. "Ready to learn about ranch work?"

"As ready as I'll ever be," Emma replied, standing. Her nerves fluttered with equal parts of excitement and apprehension.

"That's the spirit," Judd approved, easing into an armchair near the hearth in the living room with his morning paper. "Just remember—"

"Take it slow, we know, Daddy," Grace finished with fond exasperation. "Emma will be fine."

"Hold on… let me get you both some water," Linda called from the kitchen.

"Emma, don't hesitate to come in if you need a break. We're not trying to work you to death on your first day," Loretta said.

Ellie's voice drifted from the kitchen, singing what sounded like a made-up song about dish-drying and chickens. The simple joy in her voice made Emma smile.

"Best get moving," Grace said, accepting the water bottles Linda handed her. "The morning's burning daylight."

As they headed for the door, Emma took one last look at the dining room. Sunlight slanted across the well-worn table where minutes ago, a family had shared not just breakfast, but their lives, their work, their home. Something tugged at her heart—a longing she hadn't even known she carried.

"Coming?" Grace asked, holding the screen door.

Emma nodded, squaring her shoulders. Time to learn what real ranch work was all about. But as she followed Grace outside, she couldn't shake the feeling that she might be learning about far more than just horses and hay.

Chapter 5

"Hold that pitchfork like you mean business," Grace instructed, demonstrating the proper grip. "It's all in the wrists."

Emma adjusted her hold, determined to master this basic ranch tool. The scents of hay and horses surrounded them, while morning light filtered through the high windows of the arena. Her new boots squeaked with every step.

"Like this?" Emma asked, mimicking Grace's stance.

"Better. Now watch." Grace stepped into an empty stall, attacking the soiled bedding with practiced efficiency.

Emma observed carefully, noting how Grace's movements were precise and economical. No wasted energy, no unnecessary flourishes.

"Your turn," Grace said, stepping back. "Start with Thunder's stall. He's out in the pasture, so you won't have to worry about working around him."

Emma took a deep breath and stepped into the stall. The task before her was hardly glamorous, but she hadn't come here for glamour.

She'd come to learn, to understand, to grab hold of this world that called to something deep inside her.

Her first attempt sent hay flying in the wrong direction.

"Sorry!" She quickly tried to corral the scattered bedding.

Grace laughed, but it was kind rather than mocking. "We all start somewhere. Try angling the fork more—there you go. Let the tool do the work."

Emma found her rhythm gradually, satisfaction building as she figured out the proper technique. Her arms protested the unfamiliar movement, but she pressed on.

"You know," Grace said, leaning against the stall door, "we get all types of visitors here, but a successful romance author wanting to learn ranch work? This is definitely a first for us."

Emma paused, wiping her forehead with her sleeve. "I imagine you thought I'd be more interested in the scenic photo opportunities than actual work."

"The thought crossed my mind," Grace admitted. "But there's something genuine about you, Emma. I can tell you really want to learn."

"I do." Emma resumed her task, choosing her words carefully. "My readers deserve authenticity. I need to understand this lifestyle... really understand it. Not just for my books, but for myself."

"That's exactly why I've adjusted some of our usual dude ranch schedules," Grace said. "I want to make sure you get the full experience, not just the tourist version. But Emma—" She hesitated. "You did pay to be here, and I want you to enjoy yourself. If this isn't what you were expecting—"

"Grace," Emma interrupted, pausing her work to meet the other woman's eyes. "This is undoubtedly what I want. I want it all. The real thing, even the messy parts. Especially the messy parts." She gestured to her now-dusty jeans with a laugh. "Though I'll admit, I didn't expect to be quite this dirty this early in the morning."

"Welcome to ranch life." Grace grinned. "Where looking pristine lasts about thirty seconds after sunrise."

Emma returned to her task, finding satisfaction in the growing pile of clean bedding. "My agent nearly had a heart attack when I told her I was leaving traditional publishing. 'Emma,'" she mimicked in a high-pitched voice, "'you're throwing away everything you've built!' But you know what Grace? I've spent years writing what my publisher wants. It's time to write what's in my heart."

"Even if that means trading your designer shoes for mucking boots?"

"Especially then." Emma straightened, stretching her back. "Though I will keep the shoes. I'm reinventing myself, not having a personality transplant."

The sound of quick footsteps and a child's voice interrupted their conversation. "Aunt Grace! Emma! Look what I found!"

Ellie burst into the arena, something cupped carefully in her small hands. Her eyes shone with excitement.

"Ellie Walker," Grace said, "weren't you supposed to be helping Linda with the chickens?"

"I already did." Ellie opened her hands to reveal a cracked blue eggshell from a robin's egg. "It was under a plant by the garden."

Emma set her pitchfork aside and knelt at Ellie's level. "It's beautiful."

"It's so pretty," Ellie said. "Where do you think the baby bird is?"

"It's probably sitting in its nest somewhere," Emma said, thinking quickly. "Maybe waiting for its mama to bring it some food."

Ellie's eyes lit up. "Really?"

"Emma's most likely right, Ellie," Grace added. "Would you like to help us here in the arena?"

"Can I?" Ellie bounced on her toes, carefully setting the eggshell on the floor beside the stall door. "I'm really good at showing people stuff. Daddy says I'm a good teacher."

Emma smiled, returning to her task. "I could definitely use some expert advice."

"First," Ellie announced, adopting a serious expression, "you gotta have your hair tied back. Mama Loretta says loose hair in the barn is asking for trouble."

"She's right about that," Grace agreed, reaching into her pocket. "Here's a hair tie."

"I forgot all about that," Emma said as she quickly gathered her blonde waves into a practical ponytail. "Better?"

Ellie nodded approvingly. "Much better. Now, when you're mucking stalls, you gotta watch for the wet spots 'cause they're super heavy."

"Voice of experience?" Emma asked Grace with a smile.

"Let's just say Ellie learned that lesson the hard way last spring," Grace replied. "Didn't you, sweetheart?"

"My boots got stuck!" Ellie giggled. "Daddy had to pull me out after I fell right on my bottom in the yucky stuff."

Emma couldn't help laughing at the mental image. "Oh, no!"

"Oh yes," Grace confirmed. "Garrett had to carry her straight to the bathtub, boots and all."

Ellie climbed on top of a hay bale and sat, swinging her legs as she watched Emma work. "You're getting better," she announced. "But you missed a spot over there."

Emma followed Ellie's pointing finger, finding a patch of soiled bedding she'd overlooked. "Thank you, Miss Ellie. You've got sharp eyes."

"Daddy says I notice everything," Ellie said proudly. "Like how Sugar always wants an extra treat, and how Diablo pretends he doesn't care about carrots, but he really does."

Grace chuckled, returning with fresh bedding. "Ellie's our resident horse whisperer in training."

"The horses talk to me," Ellie confided to Emma. "Not with words, but with their eyes and their ears and stuff. Wyatt taught me how to understand them."

Emma spread the fresh bedding, fascinated by Ellie's innocent wisdom. "That sounds wonderful. Maybe you could teach me about that too?"

"Oh, yes!" Ellie clapped her hands. "We can start with Sugar. She's the nicest. Except when she's being stubborn. Then she's just pretending to be grumpy."

"Sounds like someone else I know," Grace teased, tweaking Ellie's braid.

"I'm never grumpy," Ellie protested. "I'm just... thinking hard sometimes."

Emma bit back a smile, recognizing the phrase as something she'd probably heard from an adult. "Well, I'd love to learn about Sugar. But first, I should finish this stall, right?"

"Right," Ellie nodded seriously. "Daddy says we always finish what we start."

"Your daddy sounds very wise," Emma said, noting how Ellie's face lit up at any mention of her father.

"He's the best," Ellie declared. "And the strongest. And fan-tab-u-lous at everything. Except maybe cooking. Mama Linda says he could burn water."

Grace laughed outright. "She's not wrong. Though he makes a decent campfire coffee."

"What's campfire coffee?" Emma asked, spreading the last of the fresh bedding.

"Only the best coffee ever," Grace explained. "Made in a tin pot over an open fire, cowboy style. Strong enough to put hair on your chest, as my daddy would say."

"That's what my daddy says about Mama Linda's cooking!" Ellie exclaimed. "Does everything put hair on your chest?"

Emma couldn't contain her laughter. "I certainly hope not. I rather like being hair-free, thank you very much."

"Me too," Ellie agreed solemnly. "Except my head. And my eyebrows. But not my chest. That would be silly."

Grace checked Emma's work in Thunder's stall, nodding with approval. "Not bad for your first try. Ready to meet Sugar?"

"Can I help? Please?" Ellie jumped down from her hay bale perch.

"As long as you stay with us," Grace agreed. "Emma needs to learn proper horse handling."

They walked together toward the pasture. The late morning air had warmed, carrying the sweet scent of summer grass. Several horses grazed peacefully behind the wooden fence, their tails swishing at flies.

"That's Sugar," Ellie pointed to a gentle-looking brown and white mare. "See her star?"

Emma noticed the distinctive marking on the horse's forehead. "She's beautiful."

"Watch how Auntie Grace calls her," Ellie whispered, clearly excited to share her knowledge.

Grace approached the fence, her movements calm and deliberate. "Sugar," she called softly, holding up a treat. The mare's ears perked forward, and she lifted her head, considering them.

"See her ears?" Ellie tugged at Emma's sleeve. "That means she's listening. And see how she's looking right at us? She's thinking about coming over."

Sugar apparently decided the treat was worth investigating. She ambled toward them, her movements relaxed and unhurried.

"The key with horses," Grace explained, "is confidence without aggression. They can sense fear, but they also know when someone's trying too hard or not sincere."

Emma nodded, absorbing the information. "Like people, in a way."

"Exactly like people," Grace agreed.

The mare reached the fence, stretching her neck to delicately accept the treat from Grace's palm.

"Can Emma give her a treat?" Ellie asked, pulling a carrot from her pocket.

Grace smiled. "Where did you get that carrot?"

"Mama Linda gave me some just for Sugar," Ellie explained. "She said it was okay."

"Alright then." Grace turned to Emma. "Hold your hand flat, palm up. Let her see the treat."

Emma accepted the carrot from Ellie, trying to mirror Grace's calm confidence. Sugar's dark eyes studied her, intelligent and assessing.

"That's it," Grace encouraged. "Just stay still and let her come to you."

Sugar's whiskers tickled Emma's palm as the mare gently took the carrot.

"She likes you!" Ellie bounced on her toes. "I can tell!"

"How can you tell?" Emma asked, genuinely curious.

"See how she's staying here? And her ears are still pointing at you, and her eyes are all softish." Ellie said. "That means she's happy."

"You really do notice everything," Emma said, impressed.

Grace unlatched the gate. "Ready to learn how to lead her?"

Emma nodded, though her stomach fluttered with nerves. This was a thousand-pound animal, after all.

"Here's the lead rope," Grace demonstrated proper handling. "Never wrap it around your hand—if something spooks her, and she bolts, you don't want to be attached."

"Voice of experience?" Emma asked, noting Grace's serious tone.

"Let's just say I learned that lesson early and painfully," Grace admitted. "Dad never let me forget it."

"Grandpa says the best lessons are the ones that leave a mark," Ellie piped up. "But I think he means in your brain, not on your body."

Grace adjusted the lead rope in Emma's hands. "Remember—confidence without tension. Sugar can feel everything through this rope."

Emma took a deep breath, consciously relaxing her shoulders while maintaining a firm grip. Sugar watched her with those intelligent eyes, seeming to assess her.

"Walk beside her shoulder," Grace instructed. "Not too far forward or back. Think of yourself as her partner, not her boss."

"Like dancing," Emma said, finding her position.

"Exactly!" Grace nodded approvingly. "Now, give her a gentle cue to walk. Just a light pressure on the lead."

Emma did as instructed, pleasantly surprised when Sugar stepped forward willingly. The massive animal moved with surprising grace, matching Emma's pace.

"You're doing it!" Ellie cheered from where she walked alongside them. "See? Sugar likes having a dance partner!"

"She's probably a better dancer than me," Emma admitted, carefully guiding Sugar through the gate.

"I doubt that," Grace said. "Garrett mentioned you were quite the dancer at your book launches."

Emma nearly stumbled. "He looked me up?"

"We all did," Grace admitted. "Those pictures from your last book launch in LA were pretty glamorous."

"That feels like a lifetime ago," Emma said, remembering the glittering parties, the endless networking, the exhausting pressure to always be "on." Sugar nudged her gently, as if sensing her shift in mood.

"Well, now you get to be glam-u-rous in a whole new way," Ellie declared, skipping ahead. "Covered in hay and horse hair!"

Emma laughed, the moment of melancholy breaking. "Is that what this is on my shirt? I thought it was a new fashion statement."

"The latest in ranch couture," Grace teased. "Now, let's get Sugar to her stall so we can teach you about grooming."

"Can I help?" Ellie asked eagerly. "I'm really good at brushing tails!"

"You can be our expert consultant," Grace agreed. "But remember what we talked about—Emma needs to learn how to do things herself."

Chapter 6

Sugar's hooves clicked softly against the arena floor as Emma guided her into the cross-ties in the grooming area. The mare stood quietly, her ears flicking occasionally toward the sounds of other horses.

"Grooming is more than just making a horse pretty," Grace explained, gathering brushes from a nearby tack box. "It's about checking their health, building trust, and establishing a bond."

"And finding all the itchy spots!" Ellie added, perched once again on a bale of hay. "Sugar likes scratches behind her ears."

Grace demonstrated the proper use of each brush, explaining the purpose of each tool. "Start with the currycomb to loosen dirt and dead hair. Work in circles, like this."

Emma followed Grace's example, carefully running the curry comb over Sugar's coat. The mare leaned into the pressure slightly, clearly enjoying the attention.

"See?" Ellie pointed excitedly. "She's telling you she likes it!"

"You're right," Emma said, gaining confidence as she worked. "It's like she's giving feedback."

"Horses are honest," Grace said, passing Emma a different brush. "They don't pretend to like something just to be polite. That's what makes earning their trust so special."

Emma worked methodically, following Grace's instructions. Despite the physical effort, she found the repetitive motions oddly soothing. Sugar's steady breathing and occasional soft nickering created a peaceful atmosphere.

"Emma?" Ellie's voice was thoughtful. "Do you talk to God when you write your books?"

The question caught Emma off guard. She paused her brushing, considering how to answer.

"I do," she said finally. "Especially when I'm struggling with a story. Sometimes I ask for help, or patience, or just... peace."

Grace nodded approvingly. "That's how my daddy taught us to work with horses. Said if you're troubled in your spirit, they'll sense it. Better to take it to the Lord first."

"My daddy says God gave us horses to teach us patience," Ellie declared. "And mility. That's a big word that means... what does that word mean?"

"Humility. Not thinking too highly of yourself," Emma finished with a smile. "Your daddy sounds pretty smart."

"He is," Ellie said proudly. "Even when he's grumpy. Or sad." Her voice dropped slightly at the last word.

Grace shot her niece a quick sympathetic look.

"Well," Emma said brightly, "I'm certainly learning humility today. Who knew grooming could be such a workout?"

"Just wait, it gets better," Grace laughed. "We could try unloading a flat bed of hay and then stacking it all or..."

"Don't scare her off just yet," a new voice called from the barn doorway. "We need all the help we can get around here."

Emma turned to find Garrett leaning against the arena's door frame.

"Daddy!" Ellie launched herself from the hay bale. "You're back! Did you bring me anything?"

"What makes you think I brought you something?" Garrett asked, catching his daughter in a quick hug.

"Because you always do," Ellie said with complete confidence.

Garrett's lips twitched. "Check my jacket pocket."

Ellie thrust her small hand into his pocket, emerging with a rainbow-swirled lollipop. "See? I knew it!" She turned to Emma triumphantly. "Daddy never forgets."

"How's the lesson going?" Garrett asked, his eyes taking in the scene.

"Emma's a natural with Sugar," Grace said. "She's got good instincts."

"Is that so?" Garrett's tone was neutral, but Emma detected a hint of skepticism.

"Sugar likes her, daddy. See her ears? They're all soft and happy," Ellie said.

Emma felt the warmth rise in her cheeks under Garrett's assessing gaze. She focused on brushing Sugar's neck, trying to project more confidence than she felt.

"The broker's interested in two of the yearlings," Garrett told Grace. "He'll be out next week to look them over."

"That's promising," Grace nodded. "Which ones?"

"The bay colt and the chestnut filly." Garrett moved further into the arena, his boots quiet on the packed earth floor. "Though we might need to adjust the price. Market's been unpredictable lately."

Emma continued grooming Sugar, but she couldn't help listening. The subtle tension in Garrett's voice spoke of concerns beyond just horse prices.

"How unpredictable?" Grace asked, her earlier cheerfulness dimming slightly.

"We'll discuss it later," Garrett said, his eyes flicking briefly to Emma.

"Don't mind me," Emma said, surprising herself by speaking up. "I'm just the city girl learning to brush a horse."

A flash of something—amusement, maybe? — crossed Garrett's face. "That so? And how's that working out for you, Ms. Carlyle?"

"Emma," she corrected automatically. "And it's... enlightening. Though I'm pretty sure I have more horse hair on me than Sugar does at this point."

"That's how you know you're doing it right," Grace laughed.

"Daddy," Ellie tugged at Garrett's sleeve. "Emma's going to write about cowboys. Real ones, not fake ones. And she's learning everything proper, just like you said people should."

"Did I say that?" Garrett asked, one eyebrow raised.

"You said people who write about ranch life should know what they're talking about," Ellie said matter-of-factly. "Emma's learning. She even mucked Thunder's stall all by herself!"

Garrett's eyes met Emma's, a hint of genuine interest flickering in their depths. "Thunder's stall, huh? That's ambitious for a first day."

"Go big or go home," Emma replied, switching brushes as Grace had shown her. "Though I'll admit, it was more challenging than writing a chapter in a book."

"Different kind of storytelling," Garrett said quietly.

"Daddy knows all about stories," Ellie announced, still working on her lollipop. "He tells the best bedtime ones. About horses and cowgirls and—"

"Ellie," Garrett interrupted gently, "don't you have a riding lesson with your grandmother soon?"

Ellie's eyes widened. "Oh! I forgot!" She turned to Emma quickly. "Will you still be here on the ranch when I'm done?"

"I'll be here," Emma assured her. "Though I might be even dirtier by then."

"That's okay. Dirt doesn't hurt." Ellie said as she ran out of the arena.

"Speaking of riding lessons," Grace said, turning to Emma with a grin before looking back at her brother. "Garrett, why don't you give Emma a beginner's lesson while I check on Carol and Tim?"

Garrett shifted his weight, clearly caught off guard by Grace's suggestion. "I've got paperwork to handle, and—"

"The paperwork can wait," Grace insisted, already backing toward the door. "Emma's here to learn, and who better to teach her than you, big brother?"

Emma felt the heat rise in her cheeks. "Really, Grace, I don't want to impose. I'm sure Mr. Walker—Garrett—has more important things to do than teach me to ride."

"Oh hush." Grace's eyes twinkled with barely concealed mischief. "Garrett would love to."

Garrett ran a hand along the back of his neck. "Well, yes, but—"

"Perfect!" Grace was practically beaming now. "I'll check on you both later!"

Before either of them could protest further, Grace disappeared through the barn door, leaving them in an awkward silence, broken only by Sugar's soft nickering.

Emma focused intently on brushing Sugar's flank, hyperaware of Garrett's presence. "You really don't have to do this. I'm sure I can learn the basics from Grace another time."

"No, it's okay," Garrett said after a moment, his deep voice surprisingly gentle. "Though I should warn you—I'm a stricter teacher than my sister."

Emma met his eyes, surprised to find a glimmer of humor there. "I can handle strict. I had a ballet instructor who made drill sergeants look lenient."

"Ballet?" His eyebrow rose slightly.

"Long story," Emma said, feeling oddly defensive. "Let's just say my mother had big dreams of raising a prima ballerina. She got a romance novelist instead."

"Life has a way of taking unexpected turns," Garrett said, and something in his tone made Emma wonder if he was speaking from experience.

Chapter 7

"You're serious about learning ranch life?" Garrett asked.

"I am. Though I'm sure I look pretty hopeless right now."

"Everyone starts somewhere." Garrett's voice held a hint of amusement. "Even I had to learn once."

"I figured you came out of the womb wearing boots and spurs," Emma said.

That earned her a low chuckle. "Not quite. Though my father might've wished it." He moved to a nearby tack room, returning with a western saddle that looked impossibly heavy. "Time to move on to the next lesson."

Emma eyed the saddle warily. "That looks complicated."

"It's not once you know what you're doing." Garrett set the saddle on a nearby rack. "First rule of riding—you take care of your tack. Check everything before it goes on the horse."

He walked her through each piece of equipment, explaining its purpose with patience that surprised her. His earlier reticence seemed to fade as he discussed something he clearly knew well and cared about.

"This is the latigo," he demonstrated, hands moving over the leather strap. "It secures the cinch. If it's not properly fastened—"

"Let me guess—I end up eating dirt?"

His lips twitched. "Something like that."

Emma ran her fingers over the worn leather, noting its smoothness. "Everything has a purpose, doesn't it? No unnecessary parts."

"Yep," Garrett said. "Form follows function. No room for extras."

Something in his tone made Emma glance up, catching an expression in his eyes she couldn't quite read before it disappeared.

"Now," he said. "Watch."

Garrett positioned the saddle pad on Sugar's back with practiced ease. "The pad needs to sit just right—too far forward or back, and it'll make the horse uncomfortable."

Emma watched his movements intently, noting how Sugar stood calmly, clearly trusting his touch. "She really respects you."

"Respect goes both ways with horses." Garrett lifted the saddle as if it weighed nothing, placing it carefully over the pad. "They know when you're genuine. When you're present with them."

Emma stepped closer, observing as he adjusted the saddle's position.

His hands stilled briefly on the leather. "Sometimes horses are easier to understand than people."

"Because they're honest?"

"Because they don't pretend to be something they're not." He began securing the cinch with swift, sure movements. "A horse will tell you exactly how it feels about you. No games, no hidden meanings."

"That sounds refreshing."

Garrett glanced at her, something flickering in his eyes. "Different from your usual world?"

"Very." Emma smiled wryly.

He nodded, testing the cinch's tightness. "Ready to learn how to mount?"

"As ready as I'll ever be." Emma squared her shoulders, fighting down a flutter of nerves.

"First, always approach from the left side," Garrett instructed. "It's tradition, but it's also what our horses expect. Put your left foot in the stirrup—"

Emma attempted to lift her foot, wobbling awkwardly. The stirrup seemed impossibly high.

"Here." Garrett moved closer, his hand steadying her elbow. "Keep your weight balanced. Don't rush it."

His touch was professional, but Emma felt a tingling sensation rush through her. She managed somehow to get her foot in the stirrup and grip the saddle horn.

"Now push up with your right leg and swing it over," Garrett directed. "The movement should be smooth—"

Emma pushed off, attempting to swing her leg over as gracefully as possible. Instead, she nearly toppled over the other side. Garrett's quick hands caught her waist, steadying her.

"Sorry!" Heat flooded her cheeks. "I promise I'm usually more coordinated than this."

"Everyone's first mount is awkward," he said, stepping back once she was stable. "The more you practice, the more natural it becomes."

Emma settled into the saddle, trying to find her balance. The height felt exhilarating, making her stomach flutter. "I feel like I'm on top of a mountain."

"Sugar's one of our shorter horses," Garrett said, amusement coloring his tone.

"You're not helping." Emma laughed.

Garrett checked her stirrup length, his movements efficient and professional. "Keep your heels down. Back straight but not stiff. Relax your shoulders."

Emma tried to follow his instructions, conscious of every muscle. "This is more complicated than writing."

"Writing seems plenty complicated to me." He adjusted her grip on the reins. "Softer with your hands. Think of the reins as a connection, not a control."

"Like a conversation?"

He nodded, pleased. "Exactly. You're not forcing, you're suggesting. Asking."

Garrett kept one hand on Sugar's lead rope while Emma adjusted to the feeling of being in the saddle. The mare stood patiently, occasionally flicking an ear back as if checking on her new rider.

"Take a deep breath," Garrett instructed. "Your tension travels right down the reins to her mouth."

Emma inhaled slowly, trying to relax her grip. "Better?"

"Getting there." He studied her position with a critical eye. "Drop your shoulders. Think about sitting deep in the saddle, like you're part of the horse."

"Part of the horse," Emma repeated, attempting to follow his guidance. "Though right now, I feel more like a sack of potatoes."

A hint of a smile touched Garrett's lips. "You're doing fine. Ready to walk?"

Emma's fingers tightened involuntarily on the reins. "I think so?"

"That didn't sound very confident."

"I'm practicing humility," she said, earning another of his quiet chuckles.

"Fair enough." Garrett adjusted her grip again, his calloused fingers gentle as they corrected her hold. "Remember—soft hands. Sugar will respond better to suggestion than force."

He began leading Sugar in a slow circle, giving Emma time to feel the horse's movement. The rhythm felt strange at first, like trying to find her balance on a rolling ship.

"Move with her," Garrett coached. "Don't fight the motion."

"I'm trying," Emma said, concentrating on staying centered. "Though I'm pretty sure I look ridiculous."

"Everyone does at first." Garrett's voice held no judgment. "My first time on a horse, I was so stiff, my dad said I looked like I'd swallowed a fence post."

Emma laughed, then quickly grabbed the saddle horn as the movement threw off her balance. "Sorry, Sugar."

The mare's ears flicked back at Emma's voice, then forward again, unconcerned.

"She knows you're learning," Garrett said. "Sugar's got the patience of a saint. It's why we use her for beginners."

"Lucky for me." Emma gradually found her rhythm as they continued circling. "This is actually starting to feel... not terrible."

"High praise indeed." Garrett's eyes crinkled slightly at the corners. "Ready to try steering?"

"What? There's more?"

"You've barely started." He stopped Sugar, moving to Emma's side. "The reins are like a telephone line between you and the horse. Pull too hard, you're shouting. Too soft, you're whispering. You want conversation."

Emma nodded, absorbing his words. "What's the horse equivalent of 'please turn left'?"

"Gently pull the left rein back toward your hip while softening your right hand," Garrett demonstrated. "At the same time, press lightly with your right leg to encourage the turn. But it's not just about your hands or legs—your whole body communicates with the horse. Where you look, how you sit, even how you breathe."

"That's... actually beautiful," Emma said softly.

Garrett glanced up at her, his expression warming. "Most people just think it's complicated."

"Oh, it's definitely that too," Emma assured him. "But there's something almost poetic about it. This wordless conversation between rider and horse."

He studied her for a moment, as if seeing her in a new light. "Try turning her toward the center of the arena."

Emma attempted to copy his earlier demonstration, relief flooding her when Sugar responded to her tentative cues. The mare's steps were measured and careful, clearly aware of her novice rider.

"Good," Garrett said. "Now try the other direction."

They continued like this, Garrett offering quiet instruction while Emma learned Sugar's responses. Gradually, Emma's movements became more natural, her confidence growing with each successful turn.

"You're a quick study," Garrett observed after she managed a relatively smooth circle.

"I have a good teacher."

Garrett ducked his head slightly, but not before Emma caught the pleased expression that crossed his face. "Ready to try without the lead rope?"

Emma's stomach did a small flip. "Already?"

"Sugar's not going anywhere." He patted the mare's neck. "And I'll be right here."

Emma took a deep breath, nodding. "Okay. But if I end up in the dirt, please don't tell anyone."

"Your secret's safe with me." Garrett unclipped the lead rope, stepping back slightly. "Remember what we practiced. Soft hands, clear intent."

Emma gathered her reins, trying to channel the confidence she usually felt behind her laptop. This was just another story, she told herself. Another scene to write, only this time with her body instead of words.

Sugar waited patiently for her cue, her ears focused forward.

"Just communicate with her," Garrett encouraged. "She knows what to do."

Emma pressed her legs gently against Sugar's sides, remembering to keep her heels down. The mare stepped forward smoothly, responding to her slight pressure on the reins.

"There you go," Garrett said. "Trust her. Trust yourself."

Sugar's steady walk carried Emma in a gentle circle around the arena. Her newfound confidence grew with each step until her left foot slipped from the stirrup.

"Oh!" Emma grabbed the saddle horn, over-correcting. The sudden movement caused Sugar to sidestep, and Emma's carefully practiced posture dissolved into what she could only imagine looked like a flailing octopus on horseback.

Garrett moved quickly to Sugar's head, but the mare had already stopped, turning her head to look at Emma as if asking what all the fuss was about.

"You okay up there?" The concern in Garrett's voice was tempered by poorly concealed amusement.

"Just practicing my rodeo routine," Emma managed, trying to regain her dignity as she searched for the wayward stirrup with her foot. "How am I doing?"

"Might want to stick to writing as a career." His shoulders shook with suppressed laughter.

"Are you laughing at me, Mr. Walker?" Emma finally caught the stirrup, settling back into a proper position.

"Wouldn't dream of it." But his eyes sparkled with mirth. "Though I have to say, that was... creative."

"I prefer to think of it as an interpretive dance on horseback." Emma patted Sugar's neck. "Sorry, girl. I promise to be less dramatic."

Sugar snorted, as if expressing doubt.

"Even the horse is judging me," Emma sighed.

"Sugar's seen worse," Garrett assured her, still fighting a smile. "Last month, Clint got his shirt caught on the saddle horn. Ended up doing a full spin before he fell off."

"Please tell me someone got that on video."

"Grace did. She threatens to post it online whenever Clint gets too cocky." Garrett stepped back, gesturing for Emma to continue. "Ready to try again? This time, maybe with less... creativity?"

Emma gathered her reins, determined to redeem herself. "You know, in the books I plan to write, the heroine will always look graceful on horseback. But maybe she should lose a stirrup or accidentally invent new dance moves, too."

"A much more realistic version of learning to ride."

"*How Not to Look Like a Complete Disaster on Horseback* 'by Emma Carlyle?" She guided Sugar into a walk, remembering to keep her heels down. "Could be a bestseller."

"*Chapter One: Why Stirrups Are Your Friends,*" Garrett suggested.

"*Chapter Two: Dignity is Overrated.*"

Their shared laughter echoed in the arena, and Emma was struck by how natural it felt, how the earlier awkwardness had melted away. She guided Sugar through another turn, smoother this time.

"Much better," Garrett approved. "You're finding your rhythm."

"I think Sugar's doing most of the work." Emma stroked the mare's neck. "She's probably wondering why she got stuck with the uncoordinated city girl."

"Actually," Garrett said, watching them move around the arena, "she's pretty content. If she didn't like you, you'd know it."

"How?"

"You'd be in that dirt you were worried about earlier."

Sugar's hooves beat a steady rhythm against the arena floor as Emma guided her in another circle.

"You're starting to look comfortable up there," Garrett observed.

"Don't jinx it." Emma focused on maintaining her posture. "The minute someone says I'm doing well, that's when disaster strikes."

"Speaking from experience?"

"Let's just say my first public speaking event involved a broken heel, an overturned podium, and my notes scattered across the stage like confetti." She guided Sugar through another turn. "I learned to never wear new shoes, especially three inch stilettos, to important events after that."

"Sounds like a story worth hearing."

Emma glanced at him, surprised by the interest in his voice. "Maybe I'll tell you sometime. If you promise not to laugh."

"Can't make that promise." His eyes held a warmth that made her breath catch. "But I might share some stories of my own mishaps in return."

"The great Garrett Walker makes mistakes? I'm shocked."

"Don't let Ellie hear you say that. She's convinced I can do anything."

Something in his tone made Emma study him more closely. "That bothers you, doesn't it?"

Garrett was quiet for a moment, adjusting Sugar's lead rope. "Sometimes... sometimes I worry about letting her down. About not being enough for her."

The vulnerability in his admission touched something in Emma's heart. "From what I've seen, you're exactly what she needs."

He glanced up, their eyes meeting. The moment stretched between them, heavy with unspoken words.

Sugar chose that moment to sneeze, breaking the spell.

"Bless you," Emma said automatically, then laughed at herself. "Do people say that to horses?"

"Ellie does." Garrett's expression softened at the mention of his daughter. "She also says 'excuse me' when Thunder burps."

"Smart girl. It's important to have good manners around livestock."

"Speaking of manners," Garrett said, "ready to learn how to properly stop?"

Emma nodded, though uncertainty flickered through her. "As long as it doesn't involve emergency brakes or airbags."

"Just gentle pressure on the reins, sitting deep in the saddle." He demonstrated the motion. "Like having a conversation, remember?"

"'Please stop' instead of 'HALT!'?"

"Exactly." He watched as she attempted the movement. "Less with your arms, more with your whole body. Think about sinking your weight down."

Emma tried again, pleased when Sugar responded with a smooth stop. "That wasn't so bad."

"Now for the dismount."

"The fun part," Emma muttered.

"Take your right foot out of the stirrup first," Garrett instructed. "Swing your leg over, then slide down. Keep hold of the reins."

Emma followed his directions, attempting to dismount with some semblance of grace. Her legs felt oddly rubbery as she landed, and she stumbled slightly.

Garrett's hands caught her elbows, steadying her. "Easy there."

"Thanks." Emma was acutely aware of his proximity, of the strength in his gentle grip. "Is it normal to feel like my legs are made of jelly?"

"The first ride uses muscles you didn't know you had." He released her arms, stepping back. "You'll feel it tomorrow."

"Something to look forward to." Emma patted Sugar's neck. "Thank you for not dumping me in the dirt, sweet girl."

"Do you always..." Emma began, but stopped when she noticed Garrett checking his watch, his posture subtly shifting.

"I'm sure Linda has delivered your lunch by now," he said, running a hand along the back of his neck. "You should find it in the fridge in your tiny home. Take a break for a while." He paused, glancing toward the door. "Grace mentioned she's taking everyone on a trail ride around two, so rest up."

Emma nodded, recognizing the polite dismissal. "Of course. Thank you for the lesson. I learned a lot."

"You did well." His words were genuine despite his apparent discomfort. "I'll take care of Sugar. Go rest."

She watched him as he guided Sugar away.

"What a puzzle he is," she thought. *"One I can't seem to figure out."*

Chapter 8

Emma settled into the cozy window seat of her tiny home, laptop balanced on her knees. The late afternoon Montana breeze drifted through the open window, carrying the distant sound of horses nickering in the pasture. Her fingers hovered over the keyboard as she contemplated how to capture her ranch experiences for her eager readers.

The blank screen of her blog dashboard stared back at her. Usually, writer's block plagued her during moments like these lately, but today the words bubbled up naturally, fueled by genuine excitement about her adventures.

She began typing:

Dear readers,

Greetings from Montana! Your favorite rom-com author has traded stilettos for cowboy boots (though not very gracefully—more on that later) and city lights for starlit skies. I've officially arrived at Silver Bluff

Ranch, where I'm immersing myself in authentic ranch life to research my new book series.

First impressions? This place is real. Not movie-set real, not Instagram-filter real, but genuinely, authentically real. The kind of real that leaves hay in your hair, dirt on your jeans, horse hair on your cute shirt, and somehow makes you feel more alive than any luxury spa day ever could.

The Walker family, who owns and operates Silver Bluff, has welcomed me with open arms. There's Grace, whose warm heart matches her name perfectly. Judd and Loretta, whose love for each other and this land radiates through everything they do. Linda, the ranch cook, whose cinnamon rolls alone are worth the trip to Montana. And then there's Garrett...

Emma paused, her fingers stilling on the keys. How to describe Garrett Walker without revealing too much of her own confusing reactions to him? She backspaced several times before continuing,

Garrett Walker runs the quarter horse operation with competence and dedication. He's been kind enough to teach me some basics of horsemanship, though I'm pretty sure he's regretting that decision after watching my less-than-graceful attempts at mounting and dismounting.

But the real star of Silver Bluff is Ellie, Garrett's daughter. This pint-sized cowgirl has appointed herself my personal ranch guide, complete with commentary on everything from proper horse-brushing technique to the naming of a barn kitten. (Yes, there are kittens. No, I'm not planning to smuggle one back to LA in my suitcase. Though I've considered it.)

Speaking of animals, I've made a new four-legged friend named Sugar. She's a patient mare who's teaching me the basics of riding, though I suspect she finds my city-girl awkwardness rather amusing. Today, during my first riding lesson, I managed to invent an entirely new form of equestrian interpretive dance when my foot slipped out of my stirrup. Sugar, bless her heart, merely turned her head to give me a look that clearly said, 'Really, human?'

But you know what? Every stumble, every mistake, every hay-covered moment feels like I'm genuinely living. There's something incredibly humbling about learning new skills, about admitting you don't know everything. And the ranch folks? They don't judge. They just help you up, dust you off, and show you how to do it better next time.

Remember how I told you I was burned out on writing? How the spark had dimmed? Well, being here, experiencing this life firsthand—it's rekindling something in me. The stories in my head are coming alive again, but different this time. Deeper. More authentic. When I write about a character mounting a horse, I know exactly how it feels when your foot misses the stirrup (embarrassing) or when you finally manage a smooth dismount (triumphant).

The ranch operates on faith, hard work, and genuine care for both people and animals. It's refreshing to be somewhere that values substance over style, where a person's word still means something, and where everyone pitches in to help each other.

Did I mention I mucked out my first stall today? For my city readers, that's a fancy way of saying I shoveled horse manure. And you know what? It was oddly satisfying. There's something therapeutic about honest physical work, about seeing immediate results from your efforts. Though I'll admit, my manicurist back in LA might need smelling salts when she sees my hands next month. (just kidding!)

Emma paused, flexing her fingers. Her nails, usually perfectly manicured, now showed the honest wear of ranch work. She smiled and continued typing.

I'm learning that ranch life isn't just about horses and cattle. It's about community—family. About faith. About finding your place in something bigger than yourself. The Walkers don't just run a ranch—they have created a home for everyone who passes through these gates, whether they're here for a week or a lifetime.

So here I am, dear readers, embarking on this new adventure. My boots are getting scuffs, (yeah me!) my jeans are dusty, and my heart is full. I can't wait to share more stories with you as I continue learning the ropes (literally—I have a lesson in lasso throwing tomorrow. Heaven help us all).

Stay tuned for more updates from Silver Bluff Ranch, where this city girl is learning that sometimes the best stories are the ones that take us completely by surprise.

With gratitude and hay in my hair,

Emma

She read over the post, making minor adjustments before hitting 'Publish.' The familiar flutter of nerves tickled her stomach—the same feeling she got every time she shared something personal with her readers.

Opening her social media apps on her cell phone, she selected a few photos she'd taken earlier: Sugar's gentle face as she had been grooming her, the view from her tiny home's porch, the barn cats curled up in the hay. She paused, studying an unposed photo Grace had secretly captured, and texted to her. At some point during her riding lesson, Grace had slipped back into the arena. The image showed Emma perched on Sugar's back while Garrett adjusted her stirrups. His expression in the photo was focused, and professional, but there was a hint of something else in his eyes that made Emma's pulse quicken.

She chose not to post that one. Some moments felt too personal to share.

Instead, she crafted a series of posts highlighting the ranch's beauty and her experiences. Her phone pinged almost immediately as responses began flowing in:

"OMG, Emma, you look so natural on that horse!"
"Those kittens! "
"Please tell me a handsome cowboy will inspire a character in your new series!"

Emma smiled at her readers' enthusiasm. One comment caught her eye:

"Loving these real, unfiltered glimpses into your ranch experience. Your joy shines through every word. Can't wait to read these new books this experience inspires!"

The comment touched something deep in Emma's heart. This was why she wrote—to connect, to share, to inspire. But now, sitting in her cozy, tiny home with the Montana sun painting the sky outside her window, she realized she might be the one being inspired.

Her phone buzzed with a text from Grace: "Trail ride in 20... don't forget!"

Emma closed her laptop, smiling.

Chapter 9

Emma adjusted Sugar's saddle, remembering Garrett's careful instructions from their earlier lesson. The mare stood quietly in the afternoon light filtering through the arena's open doors and windows, surrounded by the bustle of preparation for the trail ride.

"Like this?" she asked, glancing at Grace, who was helping Carol mount her horse nearby.

"Perfect," Grace approved. "You're catching on quick."

"She's had a good teacher," Loretta called from where she was checking Tim's stirrup length. Her knowing smile made Emma's cheeks warm.

"Daddy's the bestest teacher," Ellie declared, bouncing on her toes beside Thunder, Garrett's tall black mare.

"Best," Garrett corrected automatically, emerging from the tack room with Thunder's bridle. His eyes met Emma's briefly before focusing on his daughter. "Ellie, I'm not the best. That's your Grandpa. He's the best teacher, in my opinion. And stop bouncing around the horses, sunshine. Remember what we talked about?"

"Calm energy," Ellie recited, stilling her movements, but practically vibrating with excitement. "Daddy, can I tell Emma about the deer we might see? And the eagle's nest? And-"

"How about we let her experience it herself?" Garrett suggested, though his expression was fond. "Part of the fun is discovery."

Emma watched their interaction, struck by the easy affection between father and daughter. Even when correcting Ellie, Garrett's voice held warmth and patience.

"First trail ride?" Tim asked Emma, his nervousness evident in his tight grip on his reins.

"That obvious, huh?"

"We're all in the same boat," Carol said, adjusting her position in the saddle. "Though you seem more comfortable than us."

"Don't let appearances fool you," Emma laughed. "I'm pretty sure my heart's beating faster than Sugar's."

"You'll do fine," Grace assured them, swinging easily into her saddle. "We picked an easy trail for today—nice and flat, perfect for beginners."

Garrett lifted Ellie onto Thunder's back before mounting behind her. The little girl beamed, clearly delighted to be riding with her father. "Can we show Emma the spot where we saw the baby rabbits yesterday?"

"If they're still there," Garrett said, settling Ellie securely in front of him. "Animals don't stay in one place like people do."

"Except cows," Ellie informed Emma seriously. "They're creatures of hab... habit. That's what Grandpa says."

Emma bit back a smile as she prepared to mount Sugar, remembering her earlier awkward attempts. Before she could overthink it, she put her foot in the stirrup and swung up, managing to land somewhat gracefully in the saddle.

"Much better." Garrett's approval sent a small thrill through her.

Grace led their small group out of the arena and onto a well-worn trail that wound through a meadow dotted with summer wildflowers. The afternoon held that perfect Montana clarity—crisp air carrying the scent of sage and distant pine.

"Remember," Grace called back to their group, "stay in single file until we reach the wider trails. And no worries... the horses you are on will naturally follow each other."

Emma focused on keeping Sugar steady behind Thunder, noting how the mare seemed to relax into an easy rhythm. Ahead, Ellie's animated chatter drifted back.

"Daddy, tell Emma about the time you found the lost calf in the storm."

"I don't think Ms. Carlyle-" Garrett began.

"Emma," she corrected, earning a quick glance over his shoulder.

"I don't think Emma wants to hear old ranch stories."

"Actually, I would," Emma said, surprised by her boldness. "Research, remember?"

A ghost of a smile touched Garrett's lips. "Research."

"Please, Daddy?" Ellie twisted to look up at him. "It's a good story. With a happy ending and everything."

"Eyes forward, Ellie," Garrett reminded gently, steadying her. He was quiet for a moment, then began speaking in that deep, steady voice that Emma was growing to appreciate more and more.

"It was during the spring calving season, three years ago. We had a bad storm blow in—the kind that makes you grateful for solid walls and a warm fire."

"The wind went whoosh," Ellie added helpfully, making a sweeping gesture with her hands.

"That it did," Garrett agreed. "We'd brought most of the herd close to the barn, but one of our first-time mothers had wandered off. I found tracks leading into Miller's Grove."

"That's where the big old trees are," Ellie explained. "They're really tall, taller than our house!"

Emma nodded, genuinely invested in the story. "Did you find them?"

"Eventually. The mama cow had gotten herself stuck in some undergrowth, and her calf was barely standing. Both of them were scared and cold."

"But Daddy saved them," Ellie said proudly. "He carried the baby calf all the way back while Thunder led the mama cow home."

"Thunder's good with scared animals," Garrett said, patting the mare's neck. "Better than me sometimes."

"I doubt that," Emma said, thinking of how gentle he was with Ellie.

Garrett glanced back at her, their eyes meeting briefly. He tipped his hat before turning his attention forward once more.

"Hold up," Grace called from the front of their line. "There's a wider trail ahead. We can spread out a bit."

The path opened into a sweeping meadow, tall grass swaying in the afternoon breeze. Grace and Carol moved to one side, while Loretta and Tim took the other, leaving Emma riding beside Garrett and Ellie in the middle.

"Look!" Ellie pointed excitedly. "Prairie dogs! See their little houses?"

Emma spotted the small mounds dotting the grassland. "They live underground?"

"They're like tiny architects," Garrett explained. "Whole communities down there, with different rooms for different purposes."

"Just like people's houses," Ellie said. "Daddy, do prairie dogs watch TV?"

The question startled a laugh from Emma, and she caught Garrett fighting a smile.

"No, sunshine. They're too busy doing prairie dog things."

"Like what?"

"Standing guard, gathering food, taking care of their families."

Emma watched a prairie dog pop up from its burrow, standing at attention. "That one's definitely on guard duty."

"They take turns," Garrett said. "Always watching out for each other. When one spots danger, it warns the others."

"Smart system," Emma observed.

"God gives every creature what it needs to survive," Garrett said. "Even the smallest ones."

The simplicity of his faith touched something in Emma. She'd grown up with religion as a formal thing—Sunday best clothes and memorized prayers. This prayer at dinner. That prayer at bedtime. But here, surrounded by Montana's wild beauty, she felt closer to something real and profound. God's hand was very evident in everything that surrounded her.

Sugar's steady gait beneath her had become almost comfortable, though Emma remained aware of every step. The mare seemed to know she carried a novice rider, placing her feet with careful precision.

"You're relaxing more in the saddle," Garrett noted. "Moving more with her instead of against her."

"Sugar's doing all the work," Emma admitted. "I'm just trying not to mess up her rhythm."

"That's half the battle right there. Too many people try to force their will on a horse instead of working with them."

"Like my writing," Emma mused. "Sometimes you have to let the story lead you instead of forcing it where you think it should go."

Garrett looked at her with interest. "That happen often?"

"More than I'd like to admit. My last book..." She trailed off, remembering the endless rewrites, the growing sense of disconnection from her own words.

"Your last book?" he prompted.

"It was like trying to saddle a horse that didn't want to be caught. Everything felt forced, artificial. But I had to do it. I had signed a contract with my publisher, I had to produce what I had promised."

"That why you're changing direction? Moving to writing about ranch life?"

Emma nodded, surprised by his perception. "Partly. I need something real. Something that matters to me."

"And you think you'll find that here?"

"I already am."

Their eyes met, and Emma felt that now-familiar flutter in her chest.

"Daddy! The rabbits! Can we stop and look?"

Sure enough, a cluster of young cottontails was visible near a fallen log, their tiny forms nearly hidden in the grass.

Garrett reined Thunder to a gentle stop, Emma following suit with Sugar. The rest of their group continued ahead, Grace gesturing that they'd wait at the next bend.

"Remember to be very quiet," Garrett murmured to Ellie. "We don't want to frighten them."

Emma held her breath, watching the baby rabbits hop and play, seemingly unaware of their audience. The scene was like something from a children's book—all innocence and wonder.

"They're practicing," Ellie whispered. "Daddy says all babies have to practice to learn things."

"Your daddy's right about that," Emma said.

"Even people babies?" Ellie twisted to look up at Garrett. "Did I have to practice things?"

A shadow crossed Garrett's face. There and gone so quickly, Emma almost missed it. "You sure did, sunshine. Walking, talking, riding—you practiced it all."

"Did Mama help me practice?"

The question hung in the air, heavy. Emma's heart ached at the lost look that flickered across Garrett's features before he composed himself.

"She did," he said quietly. "She was very patient, just like these mama rabbits are with their babies."

"Mama's in heaven, Miss Emma," Ellie said matter-of-factly, with the innocent directness only a child could manage. "But Daddy says she watches over us, like the prairie dogs watch out for their families."

Emma's breath caught, understanding finally dawning. The shadows in Garrett's eyes, his guardedness, Ellie's occasional wistful comments—it all made sense now. She glanced at Garrett, who sat straight-backed in his saddle, eyes fixed on some distant point.

"I-" Emma started, then stopped, unsure what to say.

"The rabbits are leaving," Ellie observed, unaware of the weight of the moment. "Can we go catch up with Aunt Grace now?"

"Sure can, sunshine." Garrett's voice was steady, though Emma caught the slight tightening of his hands on the reins. He clicked softly to Thunder, who moved forward at an easy walk.

Sugar followed without prompting, and Emma found herself searching for the right words. 'I'm sorry' seemed inadequate, and yet staying silent felt wrong, too.

"You know what else watches over us?" Ellie asked, breaking the tension. "Angels. Pastor Sam says they're God's special helpers. Do you think they ride horses in heaven, Daddy?"

A ghost of a smile touched Garrett's lips. "Could be, sunshine. The Bible does mention white horses."

"Really?" Emma asked, genuine interest mixing with relief at the shift in conversation.

"Revelation 19," Garrett said. "Though I doubt they need saddles up there."

"Or stirrups," Emma added, thinking of her own dependence on them.

Ellie giggled. "Or helmets! Because angels can't fall off, right, Daddy?"

"I suppose not." Garrett's tension seemed to ease slightly. "Though down here, we still need to be careful."

They caught up with the others, who had paused in a shaded grove. Grace was pointing out various wildflowers to Carol, while Loretta shared a story about local wildlife with Tim.

"Everything okay back there?" Grace called, her eyes moving between Garrett and Emma.

"We saw baby rabbits!" Ellie announced before either could respond. "They were practicing hopping!"

The trail widened again as they continued. Emma found herself studying Garrett when she thought he wasn't looking, seeing him in a new light. The strength it must take to raise a child alone, to carry his grief and still answer Ellie's innocent questions...

"You're thinking awful loud over there," Garrett said, startling her.

"Sorry, I—" Emma flushed at being caught. "I was just..."

"Trying to figure out what to say?" His voice held no accusation, just a weary understanding.

"Yes," she admitted. "I don't want to say the wrong thing."

"There is no right or wrong thing to say," he said simply. "But Ellie's right. Her mama's in heaven, and we trust God's plan, even when we don't understand it."

The trail curved gently around a stand of aspens; the leaves rustling in the afternoon breeze. Emma let the peaceful sound wash over her, processing Garrett's words. His quiet faith, even in the face of such loss, struck her deeply.

"Daddy, can we show Emma the creek?" Ellie asked. "The one with the pretty rocks?"

"That's where we're headed," Grace called back. "Perfect spot for a rest."

"And snacks?" Ellie's hopeful tone made everyone chuckle.

"Yes, Ellie, Mama Linda packed something special," Loretta said. "Though knowing you, you've already figured out what it is."

"Snickerdoodles!" Ellie bounced slightly in the saddle. "I helped make them yesterday. Daddy says they're the best cookies in Montana."

"A completely unbiased opinion, I'm sure," Emma teased.

"Actually," Garrett said, that hint of a smile touching his lips again, "they won first place at the county fair last year. Ellie and Linda make quite the baking team."

"Ellie's already better at it than me," Loretta laughed. "I still can't get my snickerdoodles to turn out right."

"That's because you don't sing to them," Ellie explained seriously. "Cookies need love songs to turn out good."

Emma caught Garrett's eye, sharing a moment of amusement at Ellie's logic.

The sound of running water grew stronger, and soon the trail opened onto a small clearing beside a creek. Smooth rocks lined the bank, and the water tumbled musically over a series of small rapids.

"This is beautiful," Carol said, echoing Emma's thoughts.

"One of our favorite spots," Grace said, dismounting smoothly. "The horses can drink here, and there's plenty of shade."

Emma watched carefully as the others dismounted, determined not to repeat her earlier awkward attempts. She swung her leg over, preparing to slide down—only to find Garrett had moved Thunder closer, his hand extended to steady her if needed.

"Thanks," she said, accepting his help. His touch was brief but sure, and Emma tried to ignore the warmth that spread from where her hand had rested in his.

"Daddy, can I show Emma the special rocks?" Ellie was already scrambling down from Thunder's back into her father's waiting arms. "Please?"

"After everyone's settled," Garrett said. "Let's take care of the horses first."

Emma followed his lead in loosening Sugar's cinch and allowing her to drink from the creek. The mare lowered her head to the clear water, her movements unhurried and peaceful.

"Always horses first," Garrett explained, seeing Emma's interest. "It's not just practical—it's respect. They carry us without complaint, trust us to guide them safely. The least we can do is make sure they're comfortable before we think about ourselves."

Emma watched as Ellie crouched by the water's edge, carefully selecting rocks and showing them to Carol and Tim. The little girl's excitement was contagious, her voice carrying clearly over the creek's gentle music.

"This one's magic 'cause it sparkles," Ellie explained, holding up a stone flecked with mica. "And this one looks like a heart if you turn it just right."

"She's got quite the eye for detail," Emma said to Garrett as they spread a blanket Grace had brought in the shade of a towering cottonwood.

"Takes after her mother that way." His voice was soft, tinged with something between pride and melancholy. "Sarah was an artist. She could find beauty in the smallest things."

Emma's heart squeezed at the tenderness in his tone. Before she could respond, Loretta appeared with a small basket.

"Here we go," she announced, her cheerful voice drawing everyone closer. "Linda's famous snickerdoodles, and some of that honey lavender lemonade Grace has been raving about."

"The secret ingredient in the cookies is love songs," Ellie informed Tim solemnly as he accepted a cookie. "And cinnamon. Lots of cinnamon."

"Can't argue with that recipe," Tim laughed, relaxing for perhaps the first time since they'd started the ride.

Emma settled on the blanket, accepting a Styrofoam cup of lemonade from Grace. The sweetness was perfectly balanced, with a hint of something floral—subtle but refreshing.

"This is amazing," Carol said after a sip. "I don't suppose the recipe is shareable?"

"Family secret," Grace winked. "Though, if you'd like, we could make you an honorary part of the family."

"Speaking of family recipes," Loretta began, a mischievous glint in her eye, "Garrett, remember when you tried to make your daddy's chili recipe for the ranch hands?"

"Mother," Garrett warned, but Emma caught the slight curl of his lips.

"Oh, now this I have to hear," Emma said, unable to resist.

"Let's just say," she continued, ignoring her son's mock glare, "that we learned the difference between tablespoons and teaspoons of cayenne pepper that day."

"The ranch hands couldn't taste anything for a week," Grace added, grinning. "Wyatt still brings it up whenever Garrett tries to critique anyone's cooking."

"I was sixteen," Garrett defended, though his eyes held amusement. "And if I remember correctly, Grace, you weren't much better with your first attempt at biscuits."

"Those weren't biscuits," Loretta corrected. "They were ammunition. Could've used them for skipping stones on this very creek."

The conversation flowed easily among them, punctuated by Ellie's occasional exclamations over particularly interesting rocks she discovered. Emma found herself relaxing into the casual atmosphere, noting how different it felt from her usual literary events, where every word seemed measured and calculated.

"Miss Emma!" Ellie called, hurrying over with her hands cupped. "Look what I found!"

She opened her palms carefully to reveal a heart-shaped stone, smooth and gray, with a single stripe of quartz running through it.

"That's beautiful," Emma said sincerely. "It looks like someone drew a line right through it."

"God did," Ellie said with certainty. "He makes the prettiest rocks. You can have it if you want."

Emma glanced at Garrett, who gave a slight nod. "I'd be honored," she told Ellie. "Thank you."

"Now you'll have something to remember our trail ride," Ellie beamed. "Even when you go back to... where do you live again?"

"Los Angeles," Emma said, carefully tucking the stone into her pocket. "But I'm not going anywhere just yet."

"Good," Ellie declared. "Because Daddy still has lots to teach you about horses. And I have more rocks to find."

She skipped off toward the creek again, Carol joining her in the search, while Tim spoke with Grace about the local wildlife.

"She's got a generous heart," Emma said to Garrett.

"Too generous sometimes," he replied, watching his daughter. "We're working on finding a balance between sharing and keeping some things for herself."

"That's a hard lesson at any age."

Garrett studied her for a moment. "Speaking from experience?"

Emma twisted the empty lemonade cup in her hands. "Yes, for sure. In publishing... in Los Angeles... everything feels like a transaction sometimes. Give this to get that. Share this secret to gain that advantage. It gets exhausting."

"Is that another reason why you're making a career move?"

"Definitely." Emma said as watched the creek's flowing water. "I woke up one morning and realized I couldn't remember the last time I'd written something just because it brought me joy. Everything had become about market trends and sales projections. Whom to get to know so you gained more attention. Oh, I could go on and on."

"And now?"

"Now..." Emma smiled, thinking of her notebook filled with scribbled observations about ranch life that she had jotted down. "Now I'm remembering what it feels like to write from the heart instead of a marketing plan."

Garrett was quiet for a moment, considering her words. "Writing from the heart. That's how Sarah approached her art. She'd spend hours capturing the smallest details—a leaf's shadow, the way morning frost sparkled on fence wire. Said those moments were God's way of reminding us to pay attention."

Emma felt honored by this small glimpse into his memories. "She sounds like she really understood the soul of this place."

"She did." His voice held that mix of pride and loss again. "Taught me to see it differently, too. Before her, ranching was all about the practical—numbers, schedules, production. She showed me the poetry in it."

"Like the way the horses move together in the pasture?" Emma offered. "Or how the wind makes patterns in the grass?"

His eyes met hers, something warming in their depths. "Exactly like that."

"Daddy!" Ellie's voice carried across the clearing. "The yellow bird is back!"

Everyone turned to watch as a Western Meadowlark landed on a nearby rock, its bright breast catching the afternoon light.

"State bird of Montana," Grace explained quietly to Carol and Tim. "They have the sweetest song."

As if on cue, the bird trilled a clear, musical phrase that echoed across the water.

"It's singing a love song," Ellie declared with certainty. "Like we do for the cookies."

"More likely marking its territory," Garrett said, though his expression was fond.

"Maybe it's both," Emma suggested. "The best songs usually are."

Their eyes met again, and Emma felt a flutter in her chest.

"We should probably start heading back," Grace said, beginning to pack up their small picnic. "The afternoons can turn quickly up here. And of course, dinners at six... wouldn't want to miss whatever Linda has planned for us."

Emma noticed clouds gathering over the distant mountains, their gray masses building slowly but steadily. The breeze had picked up too, carrying the scent of approaching rain.

"Good call," Garrett agreed, standing and offering Emma a hand up from the blanket. His touch was brief but steady, and she tried to ignore how natural it felt to accept his help.

"But I haven't found enough rocks yet," Ellie protested.

"The rocks will be here next time, sunshine," Garrett assured her. "Right now, we need to get everyone back before the incoming rain."

The return to their horses was efficient, everyone moving with more confidence than they had at the start of the ride. Emma approached Sugar, who nickered softly in greeting.

"I think you've made a friend," Garrett said.

"I agree," Emma said, patting the mare's neck.

Garrett offered his assistance as Emma swung into Sugar's saddle. His touch lingered a moment longer than necessary. The approaching storm painted the sky in deepening shades of gray, but Emma barely noticed. She was too caught up in the way Garrett's presence made her feel both unsettled and anchored at the same time. As they began the ride back, Emma found herself wondering if she wasn't the only one feeling this way.

Chapter 10

Crickets hummed their evening chorus as Garrett sat on the lodge's back porch, boots propped against the weathered railing. Beyond the yard, the tiny homes dotted the landscape, two of the home's windows glowing warm against the deepening dusk.

He pulled Sarah's worn leather journal from his jacket pocket, running his thumb along its creased spine. Its pages held fragments of her life and his life—drawings, ranch notes, prayers, memories he couldn't bear to lose.

The screen door creaked behind him. Only Grace moved that quietly, a habit from childhood when they'd sneak past their father's study to raid Linda's cookie jar.

"Ellie's still sound asleep," Grace said, settling into the chair beside him. "That trail ride wore her out."

Garrett nodded, closing the journal. "She loves those late afternoon rides."

"Just like her mama did." Grace's voice held the same careful tone she used when approaching a nervous colt. "Want to talk about what's keeping you out here instead of getting some rest?"

"Nothing to talk about."

"Right." Grace stretched her legs out, mirroring his posture.

He slipped the journal back into his pocket. "Just thinking."

"You do that too much sometimes."

"Someone has to."

Grace huffed a quiet laugh. "There's the brother I know. Always carrying the weight of the world and pretending it's light as a feather."

Garrett watched a bat swoop past, its shadow barely visible against the darkening sky. In the distance, Thunder nickered from the paddock, the sound carrying clearly in the evening stillness.

"The Ranch is doing well," he said finally, attempting to change the subject. "Quarter horse program's strong. Ellie's happy. What more could I want?"

"That's not what I asked." Grace turned to face him. "Tomorrow morning, I'm taking Emma to observe the ranch hands working with the horses. Thought you might want to join us, share some of your expertise."

Something tightened in Garrett's chest at the mention of Emma's name. "Got fence lines to check. Besides, you know more about handling guests than I do."

"She's not just any guest, Garrett. There is something special about her."

He pushed back from the railing, standing abruptly. "Don't start, Grace."

"You're allowed to feel things, you know. Sarah would—"

"Don't." His voice came out rougher than intended. "Just... don't."

Grace fell silent, but he could feel her studying him. The crickets seemed louder now, their song filling the space between words left unsaid.

After a long moment, Grace spoke again, her voice gentle. "I miss her too, you know. Every single day. She was my best friend."

Garrett's shoulders tensed, then dropped. He sank back into his chair; the wood creaking beneath him. "Today... Ellie asked about her."

"Ah." Grace shifted closer. "That's what brought this on."

"She doesn't ask as often anymore." Garrett's voice roughened. "Sometimes I worry she's forgetting."

"She's not forgetting, Garrett. She's growing. There's a difference."

He pulled the journal out again, thumbing through its pages until he found Sarah's familiar sketches in the margins—quick, delicate drawings of Ellie as a baby, of sunsets over the ranch, of horses in motion.

"Sarah would've known how to answer her questions better." His thumb traced a drawing of Thunder. "She always knew the right thing to say."

"You do just fine," Grace assured him.

"Most days, I feel like I'm stumbling in the dark, hoping I don't mess up too badly."

"That's called being a parent." Grace reached over, squeezing his arm. "And you're doing better than you think."

Thunder nickered again, and Garrett found himself remembering another evening like this one, Sarah perched on the porch railing with her sketchbook, capturing the way the horses moved in the failing light.

"Emma has a gift with horses," he said, the words escaping before he could hold them back. "She sees how they move as one, understands their silent language. It's remarkable how quickly she picked up on their ability to read our thoughts, to sense our intentions. I watched her connect with Sugar from the very first moment—just like Sarah used to do."

Grace was quiet for a moment. "Is that such a bad thing?"

"Grace—"

"No, listen to me." She turned fully toward him. "Noticing similar things doesn't diminish what you had with Sarah. It just means Emma sees beauty in the same places and in the same way. That's not betrayal, Garrett, if that's what you're thinking. That's... that's a gift."

Garrett rose from his chair, restless energy coursing through him. His boots echoed against the wooden boards as he paced the length of the porch. "I'm struggling, Grace. These feelings for her... they shouldn't exist."

"Says who?"

"Says me. It's too soon."

Grace's voice softened. "Garrett, it's been three years since Sarah passed."

"I still love her," he whispered, his voice rough with emotion.

"Of course you do, and you always will. She gave you your beautiful daughter. You grew up together, shared your first love together. Those feelings don't just disappear," Grace said, her words gentle but firm.

Garrett stopped pacing, his hands gripping the porch railing. "It feels like betrayal. Since the moment I first saw Sarah, there's never been anyone else."

"This isn't about betraying Sarah. The fact that you're feeling this way is a sign of healing."

"Emma's leaving, Grace. Once she gets what she needs for her books, she goes back to her world. No point in..."

"In what?"

"In getting to know her." He braced his hands against the railing, staring out at the mountains barely visible against the night sky. "She belongs in Los Angeles, with her publishing deals and book tours and fancy world. This—" he gestured to the ranch spreading out before them, "—this isn't her life."

Grace joined him at the railing, her silence stretching between them like a taut rope.

"Anyway, the ranch is doing fine. Ellie's happy. Life's good. I'm...." Garrett straightened, squaring his shoulders.

"Lonely?" Grace supplied quietly.

"Busy," he corrected. "And content."

"Content." Grace shook her head. "Garrett Walker, you are the most stubborn man I've ever known. And considering I grew up with our father, that's saying something."

Despite himself, Garrett felt his lips twitch. "Learned from the best."

"You certainly did." Grace's voice softened. "But Daddy also taught us something else. God's plans are bigger than our fears."

"This isn't about fear."

"Isn't it?" She touched his arm.

"Grace." His voice held a warning.

"Fine." She held up her hands in surrender. "But at least join us tomorrow for another trail ride or even the morning lesson."

Garrett rubbed the back of his neck, feeling the tension there. "I told you, I've got fence lines to check."

"You're just afraid of spending time with a pretty woman, and you know it. You're afraid of feeling again."

"I'm not afraid of anything," Garrett muttered, knowing he sounded like a petulant child.

"Prove it." Grace bumped his shoulder with hers. "Nine o'clock, by the east paddock. We're starting with basic groundwork, then moving on to watching the training sessions. Me, Emma, and the ranch hands. Then at one we have roping lessons. Then at three we'll go on another trail ride."

Garrett recognized the stubborn set of his sister's jaw. It was the same expression she'd worn when convincing their father to let her start the dude ranch operation. "You're not going to let this go, are you?"

"Not a chance." She smiled. "Besides, Ellie's already excited about showing Emma 'her' foal."

"Thunder's foal," Garrett corrected automatically. "We haven't officially assigned it to anyone yet."

"Try telling that to your daughter." Grace's eyes sparkled. "You know how she gets when she sets her mind on something."

"Wonder where she gets that from," Garrett said dryly.

"Must be the Walker genes." Grace squeezed his arm once more before stepping back. "Get some rest, big brother. Tomorrow's coming, whether you're ready or not."

Garrett watched her disappear inside, the screen door clicking shut behind her. In the distance, an owl called, its lonely sound echoing across the ranch.

He pulled Sarah's journal out one last time, finding the page where she'd sketched their first Christmas with Ellie. The baby's face was captured in delicate lines, her expression one of pure joy as she batted at ornaments on the tree.

"I miss you," he whispered to the page. "Every single day."

A cool breeze stirred the air, carrying the scent of sage and prairie grass. For a moment, just a moment, he could almost imagine Sarah's answer—her gentle reminder that love wasn't meant to be hidden away like pressed flowers in a book, but lived and shared and given room to grow.

Garrett closed the journal, tucking it carefully back into his pocket.

Chapter 11

Emma balanced carefully on the sturdy fence surrounding the east paddock, watching as Wyatt worked with a young bay quarter horse. The morning sun had burned away the lingering dew, leaving the air crisp and clean. Around her, the Sapphire Mountains rose against the Montana sky.

"He's teaching the horse to respond to subtle cues," Grace explained from her perch beside Emma. "Watch how Wyatt barely moves the lead rope, but the horse follows."

The bay gelding moved in perfect sync with Wyatt's movements, its ears pricked forward in concentration. Emma leaned forward, fascinated by the silent communication between man and horse.

"It's like they're dancing," she said.

"Wyatt has a gift for reading horses. He can sense what they're thinking before they even move," Grace said as she adjusted her position on the fence.

Clint appeared at the far end of the paddock, leading another horse—this one a striking chestnut with a white blaze. The young ranch hand's movements were precise and confident.

"Is this part of their training routine?"

"Every morning," Grace nodded. "Each horse needs different handling, different approaches. It's about building trust, establishing clear communication."

Emma pulled out her small notebook, jotting down observations. "The horses seem so... willing. There's no force involved."

"That's the key." Grace's voice held pride. "Our ranch hands understand that gentleness gets better results than dominance. It's about partnership, not control."

Raven joined them at the fence, wiping her brow with a bandana. "Morning, ladies. Enjoying the show?"

"Emma's taking notes," Grace said. "Research for her books."

"Well, you picked a good morning for it." Raven grinned.

As if on cue, Wyatt clicked softly to the bay, sending him trotting to the center of the paddock. The horse moved with fluid grace, each step measured and deliberate.

"Beautiful," Emma breathed, captivated by the horse's movement.

"That's Thunder's half-brother," Grace said. "Same sire, different dam. You can see the same intelligence in his eyes."

Emma studied the bay's face, noting the same focused expression she'd seen in Thunder. "Do all your horses come from your breeding program?"

"Most of them." Grace pointed to where Clint was working with the chestnut. "See that one? His grandmother was one of our founding mares. Dad bought her at auction thirty years ago, said she had the prettiest head he'd ever seen on a quarter horse."

"Your father has quite an eye for horses," Raven commented, leaning against the fence. "Taught me a lot about breeding and training."

"Speaking of training…" Grace nudged Emma, directing her attention to where Wyatt was now demonstrating a complex ground exercise. The bay moved in perfect circles, responding to the slightest gesture.

"It's like magic," Emma said, scribbling in her notebook.

Raven chuckled. "No magic—just patience, consistency, and understanding. Every horse has a story, just like people do. Our job is to listen and respond accordingly."

"That's beautiful," Emma said sincerely. "Would you mind if I use that in my book?"

"Long as you spell my name right." Raven winked. "Though I should warn you—most of what I know about horses came from watching Garrett work with them. He's got a special touch, especially with the difficult ones."

Emma's pen paused above her notebook. "Really?"

"Oh yeah," Raven nodded. "There was this mare last spring—everyone said she was untrainable. But Garrett? He spent hours just sitting in her paddock, letting her get used to his presence. By the end of the month, she was following him around like a puppy."

"Garrett has always had that gift," Grace said. "The ability to see past the surface to what's hurting underneath."

Movement on the ridge caught Emma's attention. Against the backdrop of mountains, a lone rider appeared, a small figure seated in front of them. Even at a distance, she recognized Garrett's straight-backed posture and Ellie's excited bouncing.

"He's checking the north pasture," Grace explained, following Emma's gaze. "Ellie loves going with him on morning rounds."

Emma watched as Thunder picked his way down the gentle slope, Garrett's hand steady on the reins while his other arm kept Ellie secure. The little girl's laughter carried across the distance, pure joy in the sound.

"They're good for each other," Raven said quietly, pushing away from the fence. "Well, back to work. Those stalls won't clean themselves."

As Raven strode away, Emma's attention was drawn back to Garrett and Ellie. There was something captivating about watching them together, the easy way Garrett adjusted himself to accommodate his daughter's movements, how Ellie leaned back against him with complete trust.

"Grace..." Emma hesitated, then gathered her courage. "If this is too personal, I genuinely understand, but... what happened to Ellie's mom?"

Grace was quiet for a long moment, her eyes fixed on her brother and niece. When she spoke, her voice was soft but steady.

"Sarah had an undiagnosed heart condition. None of us knew—not even her. She was perfectly healthy, or so we thought. Always full of energy, always creating something beautiful."

Emma waited, sensing there was more to come.

"It was a Tuesday afternoon," Grace continued. "Sarah was in her art studio, working on a commission piece. Ellie was napping in the nursery next door." She drew a deep breath. "When Garrett came in for lunch, he found Ellie crying, toddling through the house. Sarah was... she was on the floor of her studio. Just like that, she was gone."

Emma's heart clenched. "Oh, Grace..."

"The doctors said it was quick, that she probably didn't suffer. But that didn't make it any easier." Grace's voice caught. "She was my best friend, you know? We did everything together. When Ellie was born, I was right there with her and Garrett."

Tears pricked at Emma's eyes. "How incredibly sad. I can't imagine losing a spouse or a parent. Ellie was so young."

Grace nodded, her eyes following Thunder's steady approach. "Barely over two years old. Young enough that her memories of Sarah are more like fragments—a laugh, the smell of paint, bedtime stories." She twisted a loose thread on her sleeve. "Sometimes that feels like a blessing and a curse all at once."

"How did Garrett cope?" Emma asked, watching as Garrett adjusted his hold on Ellie, who was pointing at something in the distance.

"One day at a time. He threw himself into caring for Ellie, into running the ranch." Grace's voice held a mix of pride and sadness. "He was determined to not let her feel the loss. Even on his worst days, he made sure Ellie knew she was loved, protected, cherished."

In the paddock, Wyatt had paused his training session, touching his hat in greeting as Garrett and Ellie drew closer. The bay horse lifted its head, nickering a greeting to Thunder.

"The hardest part was watching him close himself off," Grace continued. "Garrett's always been private, but after Sarah..." She shook her head. "It was like watching a door slowly close, day by day. He smiled for Ellie, stayed strong for all of us, but something inside him just... retreated."

Emma thought about the guarded look she often caught in Garrett's eyes, the careful way he held himself apart. "That must have been difficult to witness."

"It was." Grace's voice roughened. "Especially knowing how he used to be. Garrett was always the steady one, but he also had this... light about him. He'd tell terrible jokes at the dinner table, sing old country songs while working with the horses, debate Scripture with Dad for hours."

Thunder and his riders were close enough now that Emma could hear Ellie's excited chatter. "Look, Daddy! Miss Emma and Aunt Grace are watching the horses too!"

Garrett lifted a hand in greeting, his expression softening as Ellie bounced in the saddle. "Careful, sunshine. Remember what we talked about?"

"Stay still when we're moving," Ellie recited, immediately stilling her movements. "Sorry, Thunder."

Grace smiled at her niece's earnest apology. "That's pure Garrett right there—teaching responsibility with patience." Her expression grew thoughtful. "You know, lately I've been seeing glimpses of my brother again. The way he was before."

Emma watched as Garrett guided Thunder toward the paddock gate, his movements sure and gentle. "What do you mean?"

"Little things." Grace's voice held a note of hope. "He laughs again now at Dad's terrible jokes, really laughs, not just that polite chuckle he'd been using. I hear him whistling again while he does barn chores. Little things like that."

"It took Garrett a while to help me with things around the dude ranch," she continued. "At first, he wouldn't interact much with the guests. He'd stay up here in this area of the ranch and work. In fact, he barely acknowledged the dude ranch existed back then. But now..." She smiled softly. "He's present. Engaged. When you ask questions about the horses or the ranch, he actually answers instead of deflecting. He's come a long way. I can honestly say I witnessed a man go through deep sorrow and pain... it was absolutely heartbreaking, Emma. And somehow he held himself together and made it through. He amazes me."

Near the barn, Garrett was helping Ellie dismount, his hands steady as he swung her down. The little girl immediately ran to the fence, beaming up at them.

"Miss Emma! Did you see the baby deer? We saw three of them! They were having breakfast in the meadow!"

"Really?" Emma smiled at Ellie's enthusiasm. "What were they eating?"

"Grass and flowers! Daddy says they like the purple ones best." Ellie bounced on her toes. "Can I show you my special horse now? Please?"

Garrett appeared behind his daughter, one hand resting on her shoulder. "Ellie, remember what we discussed? Miss Emma's here to observe the training session."

"But Daddy..." Ellie's lower lip trembled slightly.

"How about after lunch?" Grace suggested. "I'm sure Emma would love to meet your special horse, then."

Ellie's face brightened. "Promise?"

"Promise," Emma said, earning a brilliant smile from the little girl.

"Okay! I'm going to help mama Linda make lunch!" Ellie hugged her father's leg quickly before darting off toward the house, her energy seemingly boundless.

"Walk, don't run," Garrett called after her, shaking his head fondly as she immediately slowed to an exaggerated walk.

Emma watched as he walked away, back toward Thunder.

Grace spoke quietly to Emma. "It was hard, watching him go through losing Sarah. But he's such a good man, Emma. The best brother anyone could ask for, the most devoted father to Ellie." She paused, watching Garrett's retreating form. "And he's almost back. I can honestly say—he's almost back."

Chapter 12

"Keep your wrist loose," Grace instructed, demonstrating the fluid motion with her own rope. "Think of it like conducting an orchestra, not wielding a hammer."

Emma adjusted her grip on the lariat, trying to mimic Grace's relaxed stance. Around them, the ranch hummed with afternoon activity—horses nickering in nearby paddocks, ranch hands calling to each other as they worked, and the distant rumble of a tractor in the hayfield.

"Like this?" Tim asked, his rope tangling the moment he attempted a swing.

"Almost." Loretta stepped forward, adjusting his hold. "You're gripping too tight. Roping's more about finesse than force."

Carol laughed as her own attempt sent the loop spinning wildly. "I think my rope has a mind of its own."

"That's normal," Grace assured them. "Everyone starts somewhere. You should've seen my brother and me when Mom and Dad first taught us. We spent more time tangled up in our ropes than catching anything."

Emma pictured a young Garrett, determined and focused, practicing until he got it right. The image made her smile.

"Speaking of my son..." Loretta's eyes tracked movement near the barn, and she let out a distinctive whistle that pierced the afternoon air.

Garrett's head lifted immediately, turning toward the sound. Even at a distance, Emma could see the automatic response—like a horse pricking its ears at a familiar call.

"Now you're in for a treat," Loretta announced to their small group. "Garrett won the roping competition at the county fair three years running when he was younger. Still holds the record for fastest calf-roping time."

Emma watched as Garrett started toward them, his stride unhurried but purposeful. She tried not to notice how his shoulders filled out his work shirt, or the way he moved with such natural confidence.

"He's got a gift for it," Grace added. "Dad always said he could read a calf's mind before it even knew which way it wanted to run."

"Mother," Garrett called as he approached, "you know that whistle carries halfway to Helena."

"Good. Means you'll always know when I need you." Loretta's eyes sparkled with mischief. "These folks could use some expert instruction in the fine art of roping. Care to demonstrate?"

Garrett surveyed their small group, his expression softening at their tangled attempts. "Looks like you've got your hands full here."

"More like the ropes have their hands full of us," Carol chuckled, working to unwind her lariat.

"Show them that trick you used to do," Grace prompted. "You know, the one..."

"The butterfly loop," Loretta interjected. "It's a lovely technique for beginners."

A knowing smile spread across Garrett's face, fully aware of what his mother and sister were asking.

"The butterfly's all about rhythm," Loretta explained to their group. "Garrett, would you mind?"

He hesitated for just a moment before accepting the rope from his mother. Emma watched as he settled into a wide-legged stance, the rope hanging loose in his grip.

"The key," Garrett said, "is to let the rope do the work. Most folks try too hard to control it."

The lariat began to move in his hands, forming graceful figure-eights that seemed to float in the air. Emma's fingers itched for her notebook, wanting to capture the precise way he handled the rope, how his movements appeared both effortless and deliberate.

"See how the loop maintains its shape?" Grace pointed out. "That's what you're aiming for."

"Though maybe start with something simpler," Loretta suggested as Garrett's demonstration grew more complex, the rope dancing through increasingly intricate patterns.

"Show off," Grace teased, earning a smile from her brother.

Tim whistled low. "That's incredible. How long did it take you to learn that?"

"Hours of practice," Garrett said simply, letting the rope settle. "Usually with Dad correcting every move until it became natural."

"Would you mind showing us the basics?" Emma asked, surprising herself with her boldness. "The proper form, I mean. For research purposes."

Amusement flickered in Garrett's eyes. "Research purposes?"

"My readers... you know," she said, feeling heat rise in her cheeks under his steady gaze.

"Can't disappoint the readers," Loretta said cheerfully. "Garrett, why don't you show Emma the proper grip while I help Carol and Tim with their technique?"

"Here," Garrett said, moving to stand beside Emma. "First, let's adjust your grip."

His presence at her shoulder sent a wave of awareness through her, but Emma forced herself to focus on his instructions rather than the warmth radiating from him.

"The rope should rest here," he demonstrated, his callused fingers adjusting her hold with careful precision. "Loose enough to flow, but secure enough to control."

Emma tried to concentrate on the weight of the lariat in her palm, not the way his hand felt against hers. "Like this?"

"Better." His voice held approval. "Now, the key is the motion. Your wrist leads, but your whole arm follows through."

He guided her through the movement, his hand ghosting over her forearm to demonstrate the proper form. Emma caught a hint of leather and hay—clean, masculine scents.

"Mind if I try?" she asked, proud that her voice remained steady despite his proximity.

Garrett stepped back, giving her space.

Emma took a breath and attempted the swing he'd shown her. The rope moved more smoothly this time, though nowhere near as gracefully as his demonstration.

"Good," he encouraged. "But relax your shoulder. You're too tense."

"Easier said than done," Emma muttered, earning a low chuckle from him.

Nearby, Carol managed to create a decent loop, drawing applause from Grace and Loretta. Tim's attempt went wild, nearly catching a passing chicken that squawked its indignation.

"Sorry!" Tim called as the bird fled, ruffled but unharmed. "I think I'll stick to writing software."

"Nonsense," Loretta declared. "You just need practice. Rome wasn't built in a day, and neither was a roper's skill."

Emma tried again, focusing on keeping her movements fluid. The rope responded better, creating a wider loop that actually maintained its shape.

"Now you're getting it," Garrett said, his voice holding that same quiet approval that made her want to earn more of it.

"She's a natural," Grace called.

Emma laughed. "Beginner's luck."

"Not luck," Garrett corrected. "You're concentrating on what you're doing, and it shows."

Loretta appeared beside them, her keen eyes taking in their proximity. "Garrett, why don't you demonstrate that forward swing? The one your father taught you?"

Emma noticed how Garrett's expression softened at the mention of his father. He accepted a fresh rope from Grace, settling into an easy stance.

"Watch his feet," Grace instructed their group. "See how he maintains his balance?"

Emma studied his form, noting how he distributed his weight. The rope began to move, cutting clean arcs through the air with a whispered swish.

"The trick," Garrett explained, his voice steady despite the complex movements, "is to feel the rhythm. Like following a dance partner's lead."

Emma gathered all her courage and began to imagine she was dancing, allowing her partner to lead. She lifted her rope, and it moved more naturally in her hands as she concentrated on Garrett's advice about rhythm. The loop swung in a wider arc, almost graceful.

"There you go," Garrett said.

A commotion near the barn drew their attention. Clint was struggling with a young horse that had spooked at something unseen.

"Excuse me," Garrett said, already moving toward the situation with fluid efficiency.

"That's Garrett for you," Loretta said fondly, watching her son go. "Always aware of everything happening on the ranch."

"Like he's got eyes in the back of his head," Grace agreed.

Emma watched as Garrett approached the nervous horse, his movements deliberate and calm. Even from a distance, she could see how the animal responded to his presence, its steps beginning to settle.

"He's so good with the difficult ones," Loretta explained, noticing Emma's interest. "Patience and understanding—that's what horses need most, just like people."

"Show me that forward swing again?" Carol asked Grace, drawing Emma's attention back to their lesson.

Grace demonstrated the movements precisely. "Keep your elbow tucked like this. You want the power to come from your whole arm, not just your wrist."

Emma tried to focus on Grace's instruction, but her eyes kept drifting to where Garrett was now running his hands down the young horse's legs, checking for any injury while speaking in low, soothing.

"The horse knows it's safe with him," Loretta said quietly beside Emma. "Animals sense these things, just like people—when someone has a gentle heart beneath a strong exterior."

Chapter 13

Emma adjusted her hat as Grace demonstrated proper rein control for their small riding group later that afternoon in the arena.

"You're all doing wonderfully," Grace called out. "Ready to hit the trails?"

Tim grinned from atop his placid bay gelding. "As long as we're not expected to rope anything."

"Your chicken-chasing days are behind you," Carol teased, earning chuckles from the group.

Emma patted Sugar's neck, feeling the mare's eager energy beneath her. The earlier roping lesson had left her with sore muscles in her arms, but also a sense of accomplishment—and lingering thoughts of Garrett's steady hands guiding her through the motions.

Grace led them toward the arena gate, explaining the afternoon's planned route. "We'll take the lower trail past the—"

The sound of hoofbeats approaching drew their attention. Garrett appeared on Thunder, his expression holding something Emma couldn't quite read.

Garrett brought Thunder alongside Sugar, his eyes meeting Emma's. "Thought you might want to see something interesting. For your books, that is, would you like to join me?"

Emma's heart quickened at the invitation, though she kept her voice casual. "What kind of interesting?"

"Ranch hands are moving cattle today. Might give you some good material for those stories you're writing."

"Go on," Grace encouraged before Emma could respond. "Tim and Carol haven't seen the west meadow yet, anyway. We'll take that route instead."

Emma looked at Garrett, noting the way he sat easily in his saddle, one hand resting on Thunder's neck. "Well, I can't pass up possible good material, can I?"

His smile was quick, but genuine. "East pasture's this way, follow me."

As they rode away from the arena, Emma heard Carol's "Oh my," followed by Grace's laughter. She felt her cheeks warm but kept her focus forward, falling into stride beside Garrett.

"Sugar's looking even more comfortable with you now," Garrett observed.

Emma smiled, running her hand along the mare's smooth neck. "We've come to an understanding. She pretends I know what I'm doing, and I give her extra treats when no one's looking."

Garrett's laugh was unexpected and rich. "Don't let Grace hear that. She's strict about the treat schedule."

"My lips are sealed." Emma paused, then added, "Though I noticed you slipping an apple to Thunder this morning."

"That's different," he said with mock seriousness. "Thunder and I have a long-standing arrangement."

Their easy banter continued as they crested a gentle rise. In the distance, dust rose from the ground as several riders moved a small herd of cattle across the landscape. The sight stopped Emma mid-sentence.

"Wow," she breathed, taking in the scene before her.

Garrett drew Thunder to a halt, and Emma followed suit with Sugar. "Wyatt's leading the move," he explained. "We're rotating them to fresh grazing land in the far north pasture."

The rhythmic movement of the cattle had a mesmerizing quality, like waves rolling across the prairie. Emma watched as Raven expertly guided her horse around the edge of the herd, keeping the cattle in a tight group.

"How many are there?" she asked.

"Twenty-eight head," Garrett replied. "We keep a small herd of cattle, mostly for the ranch's use, though we sell a few each year at market."

"And they just... follow wherever the ranch hands want them to go?"

Garrett's lips quirked. "Most of the time. Cattle have their own ideas sometimes. Watch Clint there—see how he's riding back and forth behind that red heifer? She's testing him, looking for a gap."

Emma leaned forward slightly in her saddle, noticing how the young ranch hand anticipated the cow's movements. "Again... it's like a dance between animal and human."

"That's not a bad way to put it." Garrett shifted in his saddle, getting comfortable. "Each cow has its own personality. Some are natural leaders, others like to cause trouble. Good ranch hands learn to read them."

"Just like reading horses?"

His eyes met hers briefly. "Similar principle. It's about understanding their nature, working with it instead of against it."

They watched as Wyatt directed the operation with subtle hand signals. The other ranch hands responded seamlessly, adjusting their positions to keep the herd moving north.

"Did you always know this would be your life?" Emma asked, genuinely curious.

"There was a time in high school when I thought about becoming a veterinarian."

"What changed?"

"Dad's arthritis got worse. The ranch needed me." He paused. "And honestly, I needed the ranch. After I graduated from high school, instead of going off to college, I just did what was natural to me and I have no regrets. This life—the rhythm of it, the purpose... it's me, it's just who I am. Hard to explain."

"You don't have to," Emma said. "I get it."

Thunder shifted beneath Garrett, and he stroked the horse's neck. "What about you? Always dream of being a writer?"

Emma laughed. "Actually, I wanted to be a ballerina. Had the tutu and everything."

"What happened?"

"Grew four inches in a year and lost all coordination. My poor dance teacher tried her best, but I was like a baby giraffe in toe shoes."

Garrett's chuckle was warm. "Hard to picture."

"Trust me, it wasn't pretty." Emma smiled at the memory. "But I started writing stories about a clumsy ballerina who found her own path, and well... turned out I was better with words than pirouettes."

"Your readers would agree."

Emma glanced at him, surprised.

"Your blog... you've got quite a large following. I'll admit, I read a few more of your posts the other evening." A slight flush colored his neck. "And Ellie and I found your books at the library in town. The librarian said you were quite popular."

"That's sweet." Emma felt warmth spread through her chest at the thought of Garrett being curious enough about her to read more of her blog. "Though the rom-com world, the types of books I'm known for that are, well, they are different from what I plan to write now."

"How so?"

Emma gathered her thoughts, watching as Sugar's ears flicked forward and back. "The rom-coms were fun and light-hearted, but they always felt... surface level. Fake even. Like I was skimming across the top of something deeper." She met his gaze. "Being here, seeing how people really live and work together, the true bonds between family and community—it's different. More of what I want to capture in my books. I want real-life scenarios. I want characters that are vivid and full of life and meaning."

Emma turned to look at Garrett as she continued. "I want to write stories with real heart, about people who work hard and love deeply." She gestured toward the cattle drive. "About moments like this, where the beauty isn't in fancy parties or dramatic misunderstandings, or constant funny mishaps, but in the simple truth of people living their faith and following their calling."

Garrett studied her for a moment, his expression thoughtful. "You see a lot."

"Occupational hazard," she smiled. "We writers are observers by nature."

"What else have you observed?" His tone was light, but something in his eyes made Emma's pulse quicken.

"Well... I've observed that Linda's cinnamon rolls are probably illegal in several states. They're so good. And that Ellie has everyone wrapped around her little finger, especially her father."

His smile was acknowledgment enough.

"And," Emma continued more seriously, "I've observed a family that truly loves and supports each other. It's beautiful to witness. I've observed life happening around me that is spectacular and genuine, and that is what I want for myself and my characters. I want to live a more genuine and caring life."

Thunder shifted, bringing the horses slightly closer together.

"Can I ask you something?" Garrett's voice was quieter now.

Emma nodded, noting how the sunlight caught the silver threading through his dark hair at the temples.

"Are you…" He paused, adjusting his hat. "That is, is there someone back in Los Angeles? Waiting?"

The question hung between them, weighted with unspoken meaning.

"No," Emma said. "Not anymore."

His eyes met hers, questioning.

"I was engaged," she explained. "But Liam—he wanted different things. Fame, the spotlights, the next big role. I wanted…" She gestured to the surrounding landscape. "Something more also, but I didn't realize it at the time. After a lot of soul-searching… I realized he had never been the man for me. I got so swept up in the glamour of it all and never stopped long enough to realize he didn't love me… he loved the idea of me and what I could provide for his future. I never took the time to step back and look at the bigger picture until our relationship was over."

Garrett absorbed this, his expression unreadable. "Must have been difficult."

"It was, for a while. But now?" Emma smiled, surprising herself with how genuine it felt. "Now I'm grateful. The breakup led me here to this point in my life."

In the distance, Wyatt's whistle cut through the air, directing the ranch hands to adjust the herd's direction. They watched as the cattle flowed like water around a stand of cottonwoods.

"Faith has a way of leading us where we need to be," Garrett said. "Even when the path isn't clear at first."

Their eyes met again, and Emma felt the weight of unspoken words in his gaze.

Thunder suddenly pricked her ears and turned her head toward movement in the grass. A jackrabbit burst from cover, startling both horses. Emma instinctively tightened her grip as Sugar danced sideways, but Garrett's hand was already there, steadying her reins.

"Easy," he murmured, the word meant for both horses and rider.

The moment passed, but his hand lingered near hers longer than necessary. When he finally withdrew it, Emma felt the absence like a physical thing.

"Thank you," she said.

"Anytime."

They watched as the cattle drive disappeared behind the next rise. The late afternoon light painted the landscape in rich hues, making every blade of grass and distant mountain seem more vivid.

"We should head back," Garrett said. "Ellie will be wondering where I am and probably want to take an afternoon horseback ride."

Emma nodded, gathering her reins. "She's a character. She really is a special little girl."

"She is."

They turned their horses toward home, walking side by side. Emma found herself stealing glances at Garrett's profile.

As they crested the final hill overlooking the ranch buildings, Garrett cleared his throat. "Emma?"

"Hmm?"

"Will you be joining us tonight for the campfire?" He adjusted his hat again, a gesture she was beginning to recognize as a sign of nervousness.

"I'm planning on it."

His smile was quick, but genuine. "Good. That's... good."

From the direction of the barn, Ellie's voice carried up to them. "Daddy! Miss Emma! Look what I made!"

They watched as the little girl came running toward them, waving a piece of paper, her pigtails bouncing with each step.

Garrett's expression softened with love for his daughter, but when he glanced at Emma, there was something new in his eyes—a spark of possibility, of future moments yet to unfold.

Chapter 14

Emma settled into the swing on her tiny home's porch, balancing her laptop as a cool Montana evening settled around her. The day's activities had left her muscles pleasantly tired, but her mind buzzed with insights begging to be captured.

Her hands poised over the keyboard as distant whinnies carried from the pasture. The sound made her smile, remembering how just this morning she'd watched those same horses responding to whispered commands and gentle guidance.

Opening her blog dashboard, she began to type:

Dear readers,

Today I learned that true communication doesn't always require words. I watched in awe this morning as the ranch hands worked with the horses, conducting what looked like a silent ballet of mutual trust and understanding. There were no sharp commands, no forceful corrections—just quiet patience and careful attention to every flicked ear and shifted weight.

It struck me that this is what authentic connection looks like. Not the carefully curated posts we share online or the polished personas we present to the world, but something deeper. Something real.

I've spent years crafting stories about relationships, but watching Garrett with his daughter, Ellie, showed me what genuine love looks like in action. The way he adjusts his stride to match her shorter steps, how his voice softens when he explains ranch life to her, the natural way he balances protection with allowing her to grow and learn.

But here's what really got me thinking: During our roping lesson this afternoon, I kept tensing up, trying to force the perfect loop. Bless the patient hearts of those trying to teach me today. I was reminded to relax, to find the rhythm. It wasn't until I stopped overthinking and just felt the motion that everything clicked.

Isn't that just like life? We strain and struggle, attempting to control every detail, when sometimes the best thing we can do is loosen our grip and trust the process.

I'll be honest with you all—I came to Silver Bluff Ranch looking for research material for my new books... and yes, a vacation as well. I was eager to learn about ranch life so I could write authentically about it. But what I'm discovering here goes so much deeper than just fact-gathering.

I'm learning about a way of life built on faith, family, and genuine connection. Where your word still means something. Where strength isn't measured by how much control you maintain, but by how much trust you're willing to extend.

The horses here have taught me more about authentic relationships than a dozen romance novels. They don't care about your social media following or your bestseller status. They respond to genuine presence, to patience, to earned trust.

Remember how I told you I was feeling burned out? Today I realized why. I'd been approaching my writing like those first attempts at rop-

ing—trying too hard to force the perfect story, gripping too tightly to my old formulas and expectations.

But watching these incredible quarter horses respond to the lightest touch, seeing how the Walker family works together with such natural harmony... it's changing how I think about storytelling. About life. About what really matters.

I'm discovering that sometimes the most powerful stories aren't the ones we carefully construct, but the ones that emerge naturally when we're brave enough to be present and real.

Speaking of brave—your city girl feels really good about her first roping lesson today! (There's video evidence on my Instagram, complete with my less-than-graceful attempts. You're welcome.) But you know what? Those moments of awkwardness and learning are precisely what makes this journey so real, and so amazing.

The ranch folks don't expect perfection. They value effort, honesty, and willingness to learn. Whether you're a horse learning to trust or a city girl learning to rope, they meet you where you are with patience and understanding.

I've written dozens of characters finding their way to love, but being here is teaching me what real romance looks like. It's not about grand gestures or perfect moments. It's about showing up, day after day, with an open heart and willing hands. It's about the quiet strength it takes to remain gentle, even when life has given you every reason to harden your heart.

(And no, that last part wasn't about anyone in particular. Though some of you are probably drawing your own conclusions...)

Tomorrow brings new adventures—more riding lessons, more ranch work, more opportunities to learn and grow. But tonight, I'm grateful for this porch swing (which by the way, I'm loving... I wonder if I could

*have one in LA?), this view (can you say gorgeously, breathtaking), and
the chance to share this journey with all of you.*

With gratitude (and slightly rope-burned hands),
Emma

She read through the post twice, making small adjustments before
hitting publish. Opening her phone's gallery, she selected several photos from the day: the morning training session with its misty backdrop, a shot of Thunder and his bay half-brother in the paddock, her
first successful rope loop (after about fifty failed attempts).

Her thumb hovered over a candid photo Grace had captured—Emma laughing as Garrett corrected her rope grip. Both of
them focused on the task with matching small smiles. Something
about the image made her heart skip, and she saved it to her private
folder instead of posting it.

Her social media notifications began pinging almost immediately,
as usual:

"Love seeing you embrace ranch life!"

"Those horses are gorgeous!,"

*"The way you describe everything makes me feel like I'm right there
with you!"*

*"Your social media posts feel different lately—more alive. Whatever
you're discovering out there in Montana, it's definitely working for you."*

Emma smiled, remembering Grace's words about Garrett finding
his way back to himself after loss. Maybe she was finding her way
back, too—not to whom she used to be, but to who she was meant
to become.

Movement in the yard caught her attention. She looked up to find Ellie clutching a plate of cookies.

"Mama Linda sent these over," the little girl announced. "She said writing makes people hungry."

Emma set aside her laptop. "That's very thoughtful. Would you like to share them with me?"

Ellie's face lit up. "Can I tell you about the baby deer we saw this morning?"

"I'd love that." Emma patted the seat beside her. "Come, tell me everything."

As Ellie settled in, already launching into her story with characteristic enthusiasm, Emma felt a deep sense of contentment settle over her. Her life before coming here had been about crafting perfect stories. But here, watching the sun set over the Sapphire Mountains while sharing cookies with a cherished child, she was learning to live them instead.

Chapter 15

"And then the baby deer wiggled its tail!" Ellie demonstrated with her own wiggle, nearly dropping her cookie in the process. "Daddy says that means they're happy."

Emma smiled at the child's enthusiasm, brushing cookie crumbs from her lap as the porch swing swayed gently beneath them.

"Your daddy knows a lot about animals, doesn't he?"

"Uh-huh." Ellie nodded vigorously. "He says animals talk to us if we just listen." She tilted her head, considering. "Do you to listen to animals, Miss Emma?"

"I'm learning to," Emma admitted.

"Sugar likes you," Ellie declared. "I can tell 'cause her ears get soft when you're by her."

Movement near the lodge caught Emma's attention. The back door opened, and Grace and Garrett emerged, followed by Loretta and Judd.

"I think everyone's getting ready for the campfire," Emma said, nodding toward the lodge. "Look who's coming."

Ellie's eyes lit up. "Daddy!" She hopped down from the swing, cookie forgotten in her hand, as she darted across the yard.

Emma watched as Garrett caught his daughter mid-run, swinging her up with practiced ease. She could see his smile, an unguarded expression that transformed his entire face.

Grace broke away from the group, crossing to Emma's tiny home porch. "We're getting ready to light the campfire. You joining us?"

"I wouldn't miss it." Emma stood, brushing the last cookie crumbs from her jeans.

"Bring a jacket," Grace advised. "Montana nights get chilly, even in summer."

Emma ducked inside, grabbing her denim jacket from its hook. When she emerged, Grace was waiting with a knowing smile.

"Linda's cookies found you, I see."

"Ellie was kind enough to share."

"That child would share her last cookie with a stranger," Grace said fondly.

They walked together toward the fire pit, where Judd was carefully arranging logs. Loretta had already claimed one of the sturdy Adirondack chairs, a basket of supplies for s'mores at her feet.

"Here, Emma." Loretta patted the chair beside her. "Come sit."

Grace settled into the chair on Emma's other side just as Tim and Carol approached.

"Room for two more?" Carol asked.

"Always," Loretta welcomed them. "Judd's about to work his fire-starting magic."

Emma watched as Garrett helped Ellie choose a chair across the pit, making sure she was settled before taking his seat.

"Perfect night for a campfire," Grace commented as the first flames caught, sending sparks dancing upward into the darkening sky. "Not too windy."

"Remember when you and Garrett used to sneak outside after bedtime and join the ranch hands during their campfires?" Loretta asked, her eyes twinkling. "Thinking we didn't know."

Grace laughed. "We thought we were so clever."

"You were about as subtle as a bull in a china shop every time," Judd said dryly. "Especially the night you dropped the marshmallow bag and came running back into the house and jumped into our bed."

"In my defense," Grace protested, "Garrett scared me. He said he saw a bear."

"I remember that. Garrett really did think he saw a bear, and he followed you back in the house and came running into our room telling your dad and me about it," Loretta said.

Emma smiled at the easy flow of family stories, the warmth of belonging that radiated stronger than the growing flames. Across the fire, Ellie was already eyeing the s'mores supplies with poorly concealed interest.

Loretta reached for the basket, pulling out marshmallows and roasting sticks. "Let's get these s'mores started before Miss Ellie bursts with anticipation."

Ellie bounced in her chair.

As supplies made their way around the fire, Emma listened as each person contributed to the easy conversation—Tim sharing stories about his software company's mishaps, Carol describing her work as a high school counselor. The firelight cast dancing shadows across their faces, creating an intimacy that made even relative strangers feel like old friends.

"So, Emma," Loretta said, threading a marshmallow onto her roasting stick, "Grace tells me she's been following your blog updates."

"Oh?"

"Your writing captures the ranch beautifully," Grace added. "You see things the rest of us sometimes take for granted."

"Like what?" Tim asked.

"Well, communication, for one thing. How everyone here seems to understand the animals' silent language," Emma said.

"That comes with time," Judd said, his weathered face thoughtful. "And patience."

"And plenty of mistakes," Tim added ruefully, pulling back his flaming marshmallow with a grimace.

Laughter rippled around the circle as Carol helped him extinguish the sugary torch.

"So Emma," Carol leaned forward, her eyes bright with curiosity, "I've been meaning to ask—what made you decide to try writing cowboy romance? I mean, I absolutely adore your rom-coms... I've read each one."

"Thank you, Carol. That means a lot." Emma's fingers traced the rim of her coffee cup as she gathered her thoughts. "How do I explain this?"

She took a thoughtful breath before continuing. "The truth is, my last few books... they felt hollow. Like I was just going through the motions, producing what my publisher wanted rather than what was in my heart. Don't get me wrong—those books built my career, and I'm grateful for that. But I wasn't writing my truth anymore. I was writing to meet expectations." She smiled, a hint of newfound freedom in her expression. "I've always dreamed of creating romances with more depth, stories woven with real experiences and rich, vivid descriptions. And love, of course. As for cowboys and the West," her eyes sparkled, "well, I've had a secret love affair with historical western romances for as long as I can remember, and I want to write stories like those but set in modern times."

"Aren't you scared to take such a huge leap away from your rom-com books?" Carol asked.

"Oh, I'm terrified," she admitted, wringing her hands. "But I'll never know what could happen unless I try. My publisher had their chance—I submitted proposals for my cowboy romance series through my agent months ago, and they haven't bitten. So, I'm forging my own path and self-publishing. I finally realized I have to do what's best for me, and in today's market, there are so many ways to share my work with readers. I don't want to be tied down by a contract anymore, and I certainly don't want anyone else steering my career. I want creative control over my books. And I'm tired of heavy-handed editing, leaving my stories feeling flat."

"Wow, that's... incredibly brave, Emma," Tim said, genuinely impressed. "To walk away from a successful career and start all over like that."

"Or maybe incredibly foolish," Emma countered with a self-deprecating chuckle. "Ask me again in six months when I haven't sold any books, and I'm living under a bridge."

Loretta reached over and squeezed Emma's hand. "Don't you talk like that. You've got grit, Emma Carlyle. I can see it. And you've got talent. That blog of yours and your books are proof enough of that."

"Mom's right," Grace agreed.

Garrett remained quiet, turning his marshmallow slowly over the flames, but Emma felt his gaze on her often.

"So, cowboy romance," Carol mused, drawing out the words. "What is it about cowboys?"

Emma grinned. "Well, clichés aside? There's something undeniably appealing about the whole atmosphere of the west and the wild landscape... the freedom and image it creates... but a cowboy... a man who's capable, grounded, handsome, and rugged... one who knows how to work with his hands... well, that's pretty dreamy too."

Laughter erupted again, even Garrett's lips curving into a smile this time.

"We're all capable and grounded and handy, though I don't know about the 'dreamy' part." Judd said as he winked at Loretta, earning a playful swat on the arm.

"Seriously though," Carol continued, her counselor instincts kicking in, "was there a specific... catalyst for this change, Emma? Was it just burnout from traditional publishing?"

Emma hesitated, stirring the embers with the toe of her boot. "Burnout was definitely a big part of it," she admitted. "But... there was also a personal... breakup."

"Oh, Emma, I'm sorry," Carol's voice softened with sympathy.

"It was... messy," Emma summarized, opting for brevity. "Long engagement, big plans, and then... it just imploded."

"Ouch," Tim winced, his marshmallow forgotten again.

"Double ouch," Carol agreed.

"Liam," Emma supplied the name, as if releasing a held breath. "Liam Monarch. He's... well, he's an actor." She said it as if that explained everything. "The full package. Talented, charming, devastatingly handsome... and completely self-absorbed." She managed a wry smile. "Turns out, my rom-com fantasies didn't translate so well to real life."

"Sometimes real life writes its own stories, and they aren't always rom-coms," Loretta said gently, her gaze knowing.

"Amen to that," Judd murmured beside her.

"What happened?" Grace asked, her voice low and supportive.

Emma took a deep breath, the cool night air surprisingly refreshing. "It's a long story, but the short version is... we wanted different things. I realized just how opposite we really were as individuals after the breakup. I was drowning in the Hollywood scene, the constant parties, the premieres, the manufactured drama. It wasn't me. And Liam... he thrived in it. He needed it. And he needed an Emma who was more... red carpet ready at all times, I guess." She shrugged. "I tried to be that person. But it was exhausting and inauthentic."

"Sounds suffocating," Grace commented, her brow furrowed.

"It was," Emma agreed, relieved to finally articulate it. "I lost myself there for a bit. Lost my writing mojo too. I was so busy playing a role, I forgot who I actually was."

Across the fire, Garrett was no longer roasting his marshmallow. He leaned forward, elbows on his knees, watching her with an intensity that made her stomach flip.

"So, you ran away to Montana and here you are," he stated.

Emma met his gaze, surprised by the directness. "Something like that. I needed a vacation. I needed to breathe real air, not the recycled air of the Hollywood Hills mansions. I needed to see stars that weren't on a Walk of Fame. And I needed to remember why I started writing in the first place—because I love telling stories that matter, stories that resonate."

"And you think cowboy stories resonate?" Garrett asked, a hint of a challenge in his tone now.

Emma tilted her head, a playful glint in her eyes. "Don't you think they do, Mr. Walker?"

A corner of his mouth quirked up again. "Maybe."

"They do," Loretta declared firmly. "Everybody loves a good cowboy story. Honest work, wide open spaces, men with strong values… it's timeless."

"And horses," Ellie chimed in, her marshmallow now perfectly golden brown. "Cowboys have horses!"

Everyone chuckled again. The tension Emma hadn't even realized was there easing.

"Well, I'm officially sold," Carol said, raising her half-eaten s'more in a toast. "Bring on the cowboy romance, Emma Carlyle. I'll be first in line to buy your books."

"Me too!" Loretta echoed.

"And me," Grace added, her smile warm.

"Thank you," Emma said, her heart genuinely touched by their easy acceptance and support. "That… that means a lot."

"Now, enough about sad breakups and career changes," Loretta announced, clapping her hands together. "It's campfire story time. Judd, you start. Tell Emma that one about the runaway bull and the rodeo clown."

Judd groaned good-naturedly, but settled back in his chair, launching into a rambling, hilarious tale that had them all laughing again, the flames crackling merrily as the night deepened.

As Judd's story wound down, Loretta glanced at her watch. "Oh my, look at the time. I need my beauty sleep." She stood, stretching. "Judd, are you ready to retire and leave these young folks to enjoy their campfire?"

"Sounds good to me," Judd agreed, rising beside her.

"Goodnight everyone." Loretta squeezed Emma's shoulder, then turned to Grace and Garrett. "Goodnight, you two. Don't stay up too late."

"Night, Mom, Dad," Grace and Garrett said in unison.

Carol and Tim also stirred. "Well, it's been a wonderful evening," Carol said. "Thanks for including us, Grace."

"Anytime," Grace replied. "Campfires are for sharing."

Chapter 16

The flames of the campfire had burned down to embers, and Garrett used a stick to poke the fire.

"So, what's on our agenda for tomorrow, Grace?" Emma asked.

Grace leaned forward, a hint of excitement in her voice. "Definitely a riding adventure. I'd love to take you further north of the ranch. It's beautiful up there! We can see the old, original homestead, where my parents first started the ranch when they got married, and I can tell you all about the history. Of course, Carol, Tim, and Mom are riding too, if you'd prefer to join them. But honestly, their route is less scenic, and you'd miss out on the history of this place."

"Oh!" Emma said, practically bouncing in her seat. "I am definitely up for your riding adventure."

Grace looked at Garrett. "What do you say, big brother, care to join us?"

"I'll think about it."

Ellie yawned, rubbing her eyes. "Daddy, I'm sleepy."

"I know, peanut," Garrett said softly. He scooped her up from her chair, settling her gently in his lap. She immediately nestled against him, her head drooping into his shoulder.

"She's worn out," Grace observed, watching her niece with affection.

Emma smiled, watching the tender interaction between father and daughter. "She's such a sweet child, Garrett."

"She is," Garrett agreed, his voice softening even further as he stroked Ellie's hair. "Best part of my day, every day."

Grace stretched, then glanced from Garrett to Emma, a thoughtful look in her eyes. "You know what? I think I'll take this sleepyhead inside and read her a story. Give you two a chance to... enjoy the quiet."

Garrett's eyes widened slightly, and Emma felt a blush creep up her neck.

"Oh, you don't have to," Emma protested, even as a tiny thrill of anticipation flickered within her.

"Nonsense," Grace waved away her protest. "It's late, and Ellie needs her sleep. Besides, I'm beat too." She stood, gently disentangling Ellie from Garrett's arms. "Come on, sleepy girl. Story time."

Ellie, half-asleep, murmured a sleepy "Bye, Miss Emma, night daddy" as Grace carried her toward the lodge.

"Goodnight, Ellie," Emma called, watching them go.

Garrett cleared his throat, shifting in his chair. "So," he began, his voice a little rougher than before. "Los Angeles, huh?"

"Yep. City of Angels, smog, way too many people, and overpriced lattes."

He chuckled, a low, rumbling sound that resonated deep within her. "Sounds... busy."

"Understatement of the century," Emma agreed. "Constant noise, constant motion, constant... pressure to be something you're not."

"Pressure from... Liam?" Garrett asked, his tone casual, but Emma sensed a deeper curiosity beneath the surface.

"Pressure from everyone, I think," Emma corrected. "Hollywood thrives on image. On perception. Liam was just... part of the machine. A very charming, very talented, very... demanding part of it."

"Demanding how?" Garrett pressed, his gaze unwavering.

Emma hesitated again, unsure how much to reveal, but something about Garrett's steady presence, his quiet attentiveness, felt... safe. "He... had expectations," she said carefully. "About my career, my appearance, my... availability." She cringed internally at how shallow it sounded, but it was the truth.

"Availability?" Garrett raised an eyebrow.

"Red carpet availability," Emma clarified, feeling a wave of bitterness she thought she'd buried wash over her. "Social calendar availability. His needs availability. My writing... it was always secondary. A hobby, really, in his world. Something I did in my 'spare time.'"

Garrett was silent for a moment, the only sound the gentle crackling of the embers. "Sounds like he didn't... appreciate what he had."

Emma met his gaze across the fire, surprised by the unexpected empathy in his words. "No," she said softly. "No, he didn't. And eventually, I realized I deserved to be appreciated. For who I actually am, not who someone else wanted me to be."

"Good for you," Garrett said. "Takes guts to walk away from something like that."

"More like desperation," Emma laughed humorlessly. "I was dying inside. Slowly suffocating. Liam brought on the breakup, but I also realized I needed out of the relationship as well. For my sanity, and for my soul." She hadn't intended to be so dramatic, but the words tumbled out, raw and honest.

Garrett nodded slowly, his eyes still fixed on hers, and in that moment, Emma felt truly seen. Not as Emma Carlyle, bestselling rom-com author, or Emma Carlyle, Liam Monarch's ex-fiancée, but just... Emma. A woman who had made mistakes, who had been hurt, but who was also brave enough to start again.

"So," he said after another beat of silence, shifting the conversation again, "you mentioned 'long engagement.' Were you... planning on getting married anytime soon?"

"We were," she confirmed, her voice quiet. "Big Hollywood wedding, planned for... next month, actually."

Garrett's expression didn't change, but his gaze intensified. "Next month," he repeated. "So, your break-up... it's still... pretty recent."

Nodding, Emma wrapped her arms around herself. "Ten months," she murmured. "It feels like a lifetime ago, really. Strange as it is, I don't miss him." She paused, considering. "There was no typical breakup drama on my part. It just ended. I realized later that I hadn't really loved Liam. I was caught up in the romance and a life I didn't actually want. Liam, though, played the heartbroken actor for his fans. He thrived on their sympathy, and that's when I saw I was just a prop in his image, used and discarded when he was done."

"I'm sorry that happened to you."

Emma nodded slowly, a hint of sadness in her eyes. "Isn't life strange? We get so easily pulled along by everything happening around us, especially these fabricated versions of reality we see everywhere — on our phones, in movies, everywhere. It's truly heartbreaking. It feels like people have lost touch with how to actually live, how to distance themselves from all the distractions and choose what truly resonates with them. So many have become followers in their own lives, rather than forging their own path."

Garrett poked the fire again. "It is sad. I'm glad I live where I do. I wouldn't trade all of this for anything. And what you just said about people losing touch with how to actually live... well... I agree."

The firelight cast shifting shadows across Garrett's face as he studied her. "Ten months," he said quietly. "Have you dated anyone since?"

Her breath caught at the directness of his question. "No," she answered. "What about you? Has there been... anyone since...?"

"No." His response was immediate, definitive. "Ellie's been my focus. The ranch. Trying to..." he trailed off, searching for words.

"Find your footing again?" Emma offered gently.

He nodded, something vulnerable flickering in his expression. "Three years feels like yesterday sometimes. Other days, it feels like a lifetime."

"Grief's funny that way," Emma wrapped her arms around herself, the night air growing cooler. "Time becomes... elastic."

Garrett noticed her slight shiver. Rising from his chair, he moved to the pile of wood near the fire pit. "Here, let me build this back up a bit." His movements were practiced as he arranged kindling and smaller logs.

"You don't have to—" Emma started.

"I want to," he said simply, not looking up from his task. The fire caught quickly under his attention, new flames licking upward. Instead of returning to his chair across the pit, he settled into Grace's vacated seat beside Emma.

The proximity sent her pulse racing, but she forced herself to remain still, casual. "You're pretty good at that, too. Fire-building... that is."

A hint of a smile touched his lips. "Basic ranch skill. Like roping."

"Which I'm terrible at."

"You're learning," he corrected. "Nobody's born knowing every-thing."

"Even you?"

His smile widened slightly. "Even me."

"What was she like?" Emma asked, knowing he would understand who she meant. "If... if you don't mind talking about her."

Garrett was quiet for so long, Emma thought she'd overstepped. But then he spoke, his voice low and measured. "Sarah was... light. Always smiling, always finding the good in everything. She loved the ranch, loved the horses. Especially loved teaching the summer riding programs for kids." He swallowed hard. "That's actually how we met. She came out here one summer to help with the youth programs."

"She sounds like a beautiful person."

"She was. Inside and out." He stared into the flames. "One minute she was here, the next..." He shook his head. "Sometimes I think God has a strange way of testing our faith."

Emma's heart ached for him, for the raw pain evident in his voice. Without thinking, she placed her hand on his arm. "I'm so sorry, Garrett."

He didn't pull away from her touch. Instead, he covered her hand with his own, rough calluses brushing against her skin.

"So... why don't you join Grace and me in the morning for my riding and history lesson?" She asked.

"I may just do that, Emma."

Chapter 17

Emma and Grace strolled toward the stables together after breakfast the next morning. Grace gestured skyward at a red-tailed hawk soaring in lazy circles above them.

"The amount of wildlife here is incredible," Emma marveled, tracking the bird's fluid movements against the sky.

"Just wait until you see the elk," Grace replied with an enthusiastic smile. "They're truly spectacular."

Their conversation fell silent as they stepped into the stables.

Garrett stood between two saddled horses—Thunder's dark coat gleaming in the morning light, while Sugar tossed her cream-colored head impatiently. His expression made Emma's pulse quicken.

Grace tilted her head, studying her brother. "What are you up to, Garrett?"

"Giving you the morning off," he replied, adjusting Thunder's reins. "Thought I might give Emma her lesson today." His eyes met Emma's. "If that's alright with you?"

Emma's breath caught at the question in his gaze. "I'd like that."

Grace's smile widened. "Well then, I guess I'll catch up on some paperwork." She squeezed Emma's arm.

As Grace headed back toward the lodge, Emma approached Sugar, running her hand along the mare's neck. "You didn't have to saddle her for me. I would have tried to do it myself."

"I wanted to." Garrett checked Sugar's cinch one last time. "Besides, it gave me a chance to make sure everything's properly adjusted for the terrain we'll be covering."

"Challenging terrain?" Emma tried to keep the nervousness from her voice.

"Nothing you can't handle," he assured her, his voice steady and confident. "Just some gentle slopes and a few rocky patches. Remember... trust your horse—Sugar knows what she's doing."

He offered his cupped hands to give her a boost into the saddle. Emma placed her boot in his grip, grateful for the support as she swung up. His hands steadied her briefly at her waist.

"Thanks," she managed, settling into the saddle and gathering her reins.

Garrett mounted Thunder with ease. "Ready to see some of the most beautiful parts of Silver Bluff Ranch?"

Emma nodded, excitement replacing her earlier nerves. "Lead the way."

They rode at an easy walk, Garrett guiding them past the training paddocks and toward a trail that wound up into the foothills. Emma relaxed into Sugar's smooth gait, appreciating how the mare responded to the lightest touch.

"You're almost a pro now," Garrett observed. "More confident in the saddle."

She smiled. "I still feel like I have so much to learn."

"That's the thing about ranching—there's always more to learn. Even after a lifetime of it." He gestured toward the trail ahead. "We'll take it slow up this first stretch. Keep your weight balanced and let Sugar pick her path."

The trail began to climb, not steep, but enough that Emma had to adjust her position and felt a bit nervous. Sugar moved surely beneath her, picking her way between scattered rocks with careful steps.

"That's it," Garrett encouraged. "You're doing fine."

They continued upward, the morning sun warming their backs. Emma admired how naturally Garrett moved with Thunder, how his quiet strength seemed to extend to everything around him.

When they crested the hill, Emma gasped. Before them stretched a wide plateau, cradled by mountains that seemed close enough to touch. Wildflowers dotted the grass in purple and gold patches, and in the center of it all stood a small cabin, its weathered logs telling stories of years gone by.

"Oh," she breathed. "It's beautiful."

Garrett guided Thunder closer to the cabin, his expression softening as he surveyed the land. "This is where it all started. The very first Silver Bluff homestead."

Emma followed his lead, taking in every detail. The cabin's rough-hewn logs had weathered to a silvery gray, and though small, it possessed a quiet dignity. A weathered porch wrapped around the front and two sides, and an old stone chimney stood sentinel at one end.

"It's perfect," she said. "Like something from a dream."

Garrett dismounted, tethering Thunder to a sturdy hitching post. He reached up to help Emma down, his hands strong and steady at her waist. She tried to ignore the flutter in her stomach at his touch.

"My dad bought this land when he was just nineteen," Garrett began, securing the horses. "He'd been working since he was fourteen, saving every penny. Most folks thought he was crazy, buying such rough terrain, but he had faith."

Emma followed him onto the porch, the old boards creaking softly beneath their boots. "He saw something they didn't?"

"He saw possibility." Garrett ran his hand along the cabin's wall, touching the logs with reverence. "And he saw a future with my mother. They'd been sweethearts since high school, but Dad wanted to have something solid to offer her before he proposed."

"So he built this cabin?"

"Him and his father and brothers." Garrett smiled. "Took them almost three months. They'd work their regular jobs during the day, then come up here evenings and weekends. Mom knew he was building something, but Dad managed to keep the details secret."

He pushed open the cabin door, which swung with surprising smoothness on its hinges. "Grace and I try to keep it maintained. Feels important, you know?"

Emma stepped inside, letting her eyes adjust to the dimmer light. The cabin was simple but beautifully crafted—one main room with a small kitchen area, a sleeping loft above. A stone fireplace dominated one wall, and windows framed stunning views of the mountains.

"When it was finished," Garrett continued, "Dad brought Mom up here on horseback, just like we came today. Told her he had something to show her." His voice grew softer, more reflective. "He set up a picnic on the porch, and after they'd eaten, he got down on one knee right there and asked her to build a life with him."

"What did she say?" Emma asked, though she knew the answer.

Garrett's laugh was warm. "She said she'd been waiting months for him to ask, and if he'd taken any longer, she might have proposed herself."

Emma smiled, picturing a young Loretta, full of sass and spirit. "That sounds like her."

"They were married right out there," Garrett gestured through the window to a flat stretch of ground where wildflowers bloomed. "Simple ceremony, just family and close friends. Mom says it was perfect." He paused, his expression distant. "Sarah and I talked about renewing our vows up here someday..."

Without thinking, Emma reached out, touching his arm gently. "I'm sorry, Garrett."

He covered her hand with his own, the gesture achingly tender. "Don't be. Those memories of my time with Sarah... they're precious. Even the ones that hurt." His eyes met hers, vulnerability mixing with something deeper. "You know what I've learned? Love leaves marks on our hearts. Sometimes they're scars, but they're also proof that the love was real."

Emma's breath caught at the raw honesty in his voice. "That's beautiful."

"It's true." His thumb traced small circles on her hand, sending shivers up her arm. "For a long time, I thought feeling anything new would somehow... dishonor those memories."

Garrett drew a deep breath, his hand still covering hers. "Lately, I've been remembering something my dad told me after Sarah passed. He said, 'Son, God doesn't give us hearts with limited capacity for love. When He heals our broken places, He makes room for more.'"

Emma felt tears prick at her eyes. "Your father is so wise."

"He is." Garrett's voice grew thoughtful. "You know what else he told me? That sometimes God's greatest blessings come disguised as challenges. Things that push us out of our comfort zones make us question our carefully laid plans."

Emma found herself thinking of her own journey—how leaving behind her comfortable life in Los Angeles had led her here, to this moment.

"Like a city girl showing up at a dude ranch?" she asked, attempting to lighten the moment even as her pulse raced.

His answering smile was warm. "Something like that."

A breeze whispered through the cabin's open door, carrying the sweet scent of wildflowers. Outside, one of the horses nickered softly.

"We should probably check on them," Garrett said, though he made no move to release her hand.

"Probably," Emma agreed, equally reluctant to break the moment.

Finally, Garrett stepped back, gesturing toward the door. "There's something else I'd like to show you."

They emerged onto the porch. Garrett led her to the far corner, pointing to a series of marks carved into one of the support posts.

"Look here."

Emma leaned closer, making out dates and heights marked in the wood. "Growth charts?"

"Family history." Garrett traced one of the marks with his finger. "This one's Grace when she was two. This is me at seven." He smiled. "And this one... this is Ellie from last summer."

Emma's heart melted at the image of Garrett measuring his daughter against the same post where his own height had been recorded decades ago. "You're keeping the tradition alive."

"Trying to." He said.

They descended the porch steps. Garrett steadied Emma as she mounted Sugar, then hoisted himself onto Thunder's muscular back.

"Where to now?" Emma asked, settling into her saddle.

"There's a river that marks the property line," he said. "I'd like to show it to you."

They rode along a trail that wound through stands of aspen trees, their leaves whispering in the breeze.

"The river's just ahead," he said, gesturing toward a sound that had been growing steadily louder. "We'll stop at the overlook—it's another great view of the property."

As they emerged from the trees, Emma caught her breath. The river curved below them like a silvery blue ribbon, cutting through rocky banks before disappearing into a grove of towering pines. Mountains rose beyond, their peaks still holding patches of snow despite the summer warmth.

"This is incredible," she said, drinking in the sight.

"Dad says this view sealed the deal for him," Garrett replied, a note of pride in his voice. "He knew the moment he saw it that this land was meant to be home."

They dismounted at a natural clearing, and Garrett helped Emma down, his hands lingering at her waist a moment longer than necessary. He secured the horses to a nearby tree, then led her to a flat boulder that seemed perfectly placed for viewing the panorama before them.

"The river's our natural boundary," he explained as they settled on the sun-warmed stone. "But it's more than that. It's life for the ranch—water for the stock, irrigation for the hayfields."

Emma noticed how his entire demeanor changed when he spoke about the ranch, passion lighting his features. "You really love this place, don't you?"

"It's in my blood," he admitted. "Every rock, every tree, every bend in that river—they're all part of who I am." He glanced at her. "Does that sound ridiculous?"

"Not at all," she assured him. "It sounds... real. Beautiful. Everything here is so genuine, so..." She searched for the right word. "Unvarnished."

"Unlike Los Angeles?" There was no judgment in his tone, only curiosity.

"Exactly unlike Los Angeles." Emma drew her knees-up, wrapping her arms around them. "Out there, everything's carefully curated, filtered, staged for maximum impact. Here..." She gestured at the wild beauty surrounding them. "Here, things just are what they are. There's something incredibly freeing about that."

"Why do you live in Los Angeles? What's kept you from moving somewhere else?"

"Good question. Honestly, I never gave it much thought until after Liam and I broke up. That's when I started realizing I didn't love LA. I grew up there, so it was just... normal. But the older I got, the more I understood it wasn't for me."

"You grew up there? Are your parents still in the area?"

"Yes," she lowered her gaze thoughtfully. "My parents are movie producers, and I grew up immersed in everything Hollywood had to offer. While I love them dearly, age has brought me clarity—the lifestyle I maintained, even after my books became bestsellers and granted me independence, never truly felt authentic to who I am. I wish I'd taken the time back then to reflect on where I wanted to be and who I wanted to become, rather than simply staying in my comfort zone. But wisdom comes with time, and now I've finally stepped back to evaluate my life. Besides building my career, I realize I never really took control of my own path. Los Angeles isn't my future anymore. I long for a place where I can truly breathe, where my front door doesn't open to a wall of neighbors, where I can work outdoors and write the stories that speak to my heart without the constant buzz of city life drowning out my thoughts. Does that make sense?"

"It does."

"Other than thinking you wanted to become a veterinarian before you graduated from high school... you never once dreamed of a life beyond this ranch? Never wondered what waited for you past Montana's borders?"

"Never. I knew this is where I was meant to be."

A horse nickered behind them, breaking the moment. Emma looked away, thinking.

"We should probably head back," Garrett said. "Grace will be wondering where we've gotten off to."

"Probably," Emma agreed, but she remained seated, savoring the peaceful atmosphere.

Thunder stamped a hoof impatiently, and Garrett chuckled. "Someone's ready for her lunch."

They stood, and Emma found herself reluctant to leave this magical spot. As if reading her thoughts, Garrett said, "We can come back another time."

The promise in his words sent a warm thrill through her. "I'd like that."

He helped her mount Sugar, his strong hands steady and sure. As they started back down the trail, Emma noticed how the terrain seemed less intimidating now, her confidence in both her horse and her guide having grown.

"On the way back, can we ride past your parents' first home again?"

"Sure," he replied.

As they neared the old homestead, Emma's eyes landed on something she hadn't noticed before—a cross, weathered but well cared for, standing tall on the mountainside. She slowed her horse and pointed. "What's the story behind the cross?"

Garrett followed her gaze, his expression thoughtful. "Dad built that cross just before he proposed to Mom. He wanted it to be the first thing he saw every morning through the loft window—a daily reminder to keep his faith strong and love unconditionally."

Emma took in the simple yet powerful symbol, her heart stirring. She turned to Garrett. "Isn't it amazing? How one moment, one choice, can change everything. A single leap of faith... a decision made in a moment of clarity... can alter the course of a life."

Garrett guided Thunder closer to Sugar, his voice steady. "Yeah. That's what Dad always says about buying this land. He felt God leading him here, even when everyone else thought he was crazy." He glanced over at her, a small, knowing smile playing at his lips. "Sometimes the right path isn't the obvious one."

Emma let his words settle, her mind drifting to her own journey—walking away from her successful rom-com career, leaving behind the safety of traditional publishing, stepping into the unknown in Montana on a whim

"No," she murmured, her voice quiet but certain. "Sometimes it's the one that scares a person the most."

"Can I take a minute... just to walk around?"

"Sure. Let me give you a hand..." he said as she swung her leg over Sugar and dismounted.

She looked up at him and smiled. "I got this, cowboy."

Garrett watched her meandering through the meadow, where she paused to admire the wildflowers, occasionally stooping to inhale their sweet fragrance. When she returned to the cabin's porch, her fingers traced the weathered surface of the rough-hewn logs. A gentle smile crossed her face as she knelt beside the height marks he'd shown her earlier—the carved lines that chronicled his, Grace's, and Ellie's growth through the years.

She wandered back off the porch and stood, looking at the vast landscape around her.

"What do you see?" he asked.

Emma strode back toward him. With determination, she mounted her horse in one fluid motion that surprised him. She sat there for a moment, her gaze fixed on the house.

She turned to him, her eyes meeting his. "Clearly, Garrett. I see everything more clearly now."

Chapter 18

Emma balanced her notepad on her knee, pausing to capture a fresh thought before it could slip away. The gentle creak of the porch swing provided a soothing backdrop as her pen flew across the page, filling it with ideas that felt more authentic than anything she'd ever written.

Her laptop sat open beside her, its cursor blinking on a blank document titled "Silver Creek Hearts—Book 1." But for now, she preferred the simplicity of pen and paper, letting her thoughts flow freely as she reimagined her debut cowboy romance.

"This is all wrong," she muttered, crossing out her previous outline. "The heroine wouldn't be a tourist. She'd be..." Emma tapped her pen against the pad, thinking.

"A former barrel racer. Someone who understands horses but left that world behind to come home."

She glanced up as laughter drifted across the yard. Loretta was attempting to demonstrate proper roping techniques to Carol, while Tim offered commentary that had both of them dissolving into giggles. The scene sparked another note:

"Community—not just romance, but family. The way everyone looks out for each other. Fun... innocent fun and interaction. Living in the moment."

The morning's ride with Garrett had shifted something in her perspective. The old homestead, the stories of his parents, the quiet strength of the family legacy—it all pointed to deeper themes than she'd initially planned.

Emma flipped to a fresh page, writing quickly,

"Theme: Finding your true path isn't always about discovering something new. Sometimes it's about returning to what your heart already knows."

The steady rhythm of hoofbeats drew her attention. Garrett approached on Thunder, confidence in his posture.

He dismounted smoothly, leading Thunder to the hitching post before approaching the porch steps. His Stetson came off as he reached the bottom step, and Emma noticed how he turned it in his hands.

"Sorry to interrupt your writing," he said, his voice carrying that gentle roughness she'd grown fond of.

"No worries." Emma set her notepad aside. "Just working through some new ideas. Completely reimagining my first novel for the series, actually."

Garrett nodded, his gaze dropping to study the weathered boards beneath his boots. The nervous energy radiating from him was so unlike his usual steady presence that Emma felt her pulse quicken with anticipation.

"Garrett? What is it?"

He looked up, meeting her eyes with an earnestness that made her breath catch. "I'm nervous about this, and I don't want to mess it up, but..." He took a deep breath. "Would you go out to dinner this evening with me?"

A warm smile spread across Emma's face, joy bubbling up inside her. "Of course. I'd love to."

The tension in his shoulders eased visibly. "Yeah?"

"Yeah."

"Would five this evening work?"

"Perfect," she agreed, watching as relief and happiness transformed his expression.

He turned toward Thunder, then paused as Emma stood quickly. "Wait! What kind of dinner is this? I didn't exactly pack for fine dining—just jeans, shirts, and a couple of sundresses."

Garrett smiled. "Wear whatever makes you comfortable, Emma. No need to fuss."

She watched him mount up, her heart light in her chest. Thunder pranced a bit, picking up on his rider's good mood, and Garrett tipped his hat to her before turning toward the barn.

Emma sank back into the porch swing, her grin threatening to split her face. Her notepad caught her eye, and she picked it up, adding one more line to her story notes.

"Maybe weave something like this into the novel: Love shows up when you stop trying to script it perfectly and just let your heart lead the way."

The laptop's notification chime pulled Emma from her reverie. Her agent's name in the subject line caught her attention: "Urgent—Major Publishing Opportunity."

Emma clicked open the email, her eyes widening as she read:

Dear Emma,

I hope this finds you well. Your social media presence and blog posts about ranch life have garnered significant attention—not just from readers, but from Preston House Publishing as well. They're impressed with your following and the authentic content you're creating.

They've authorized me to present you with a five-book contract for your upcoming cowboy romance series. The advance would be substantial, and they're prepared to fast-track the first book for a spring release.

Please call me as soon as possible to discuss details. This could be exactly the fresh start you've been looking for.

Best,

Marjorie

Emma leaned back in the swing, her thoughts churning. The validation felt good—wonderful, even. Her former publishing house had dismissed her genre switch as career suicide, but now they were scrambling to capitalize on her potential success.

She ran her fingers along the edges of her notepad, thinking of the stories taking shape within its pages. Raw, honest tales of love and faith, family legacy and finding home. Stories that didn't fit neatly into market trends or publishing forecasts.

The security of a traditional contract beckoned—guaranteed income, professional marketing, established distribution channels. But with that security came familiar constraints: strict deadlines, mandated plot points, covers designed to match current trends rather than capture the heart of her stories.

Emma opened a fresh email.

Dear Marjorie,

Thank you for bringing this opportunity to my attention. I'm genuinely flattered by Preston House's interest and appreciate their faith in my new direction.

However, I need to decline at this time. I'm grateful for all I've learned about traditional publishing while working with your company, but I believe self-publishing is the right path for these new stories. I'm committed to maintaining creative independence with this series.

Best regards,

Emma

She hit send before doubt could creep in, then closed her laptop with a decisive click.

Her heart felt lighter, clearer, and she knew this riskier path was the right one.

Chapter 19

Emma stepped carefully onto the running board of Garrett's black pickup truck, his strong hand steady at her elbow as she settled into the passenger seat. The floral sundress she'd chosen rustled softly against the leather upholstery.

"Thank you," she said as he closed her door, noting how his black denim shirt complemented his tall frame as he walked around to the driver's side.

Garrett slid behind the wheel, his Stetson brushing the roof before he adjusted it slightly. "You look beautiful," he said quietly, starting the engine.

Emma smoothed her dress, fighting a blush. "You clean up pretty well yourself, cowboy."

The truck rumbled down the ranch's long driveway, early evening shadows stretching across the gravel. Emma watched Garrett's capable hands on the steering wheel, remembering how they'd felt helping her mount Sugar that morning.

"So," she ventured, "are you going to tell me where we're headed?"

A small smile played at the corners of his mouth. "The Silver Spur. Best steakhouse in Riverbend Valley."

"That's not saying much if it's the only steakhouse in Riverbend Valley," Emma teased.

Garrett chuckled, the sound warming her heart. "Fair point. But trust me—their rib eye would hold its own anywhere."

"I read about this restaurant online... line dancing, and a large dance floor, right?"

"Every Friday and Saturday night." He glanced at her. "Don't tell me you're scared of a little two-step?"

"Terrified," Emma admitted. "Though after learning to ride horses, maybe a two-step won't seem so daunting."

"You've done fine with the horses."

"Says the man who watched me nearly fall off Sugar my first day."

"Key word being 'nearly,'" Garrett pointed out. "You stayed on."

They passed the "Welcome to Riverbend Valley" sign, its wooden posts weathered by the Montana seasons. The town spread before them, streetlights beginning to twinkle in the approaching dusk.

"Did you come to this restaurant a lot growing up?" Emma asked.

"Mom and Dad would bring us for special occasions. Birthdays, good report cards." His expression softened with memory. "Sarah and I had our first date here."

Emma's heart squeezed at the quiet admission. "Thank you for sharing that with me."

He nodded, eyes on the road. "It's getting easier, talking about her. Especially with you."

The simple honesty in his words touched something deep within her. Before she could respond, Garrett's phone rang through the truck's speakers, Grace's name appearing on the display.

Garrett pressed the steering wheel button. "Hey, Grace."

"Garrett." His sister's voice carried an edge of worry that made Emma sit straighter. "I'm so sorry to interrupt, but you need to come back. It's Thunder."

Garrett's jaw tightened. "What's wrong?"

"She's down in her stall. We can't get her up, and she's showing signs of colic. Dad's with her now, but-"

"I'm turning around," Garrett cut in, already scanning for a place to make a U-turn. "Tell Dad I'll be there in fifteen minutes."

"Drive safe," Grace said before disconnecting.

Garrett executed a quick turn in an empty parking lot, his movements controlled but urgent. Emma could see the tension in his shoulders, the way his hands gripped the wheel.

"I'm so sorry, Emma. I need to-"

"Of course you do," she interrupted gently. "Thunder needs you."

He shot her a grateful look. "Colic can be serious in horses. Sometimes fatal if not caught early enough."

"It's fine." She reached over and squeezed his arm. "You can make it up to me another time."

The truck accelerated smoothly, eating up the miles back to Silver Bluff. Emma studied Garrett's profile, seeing the worry he was trying to hide.

"Thunder's been with you a long time?"

"Eight years." Garrett's voice carried equal measures of pride and concern. "Trained her myself from a two-year-old. She's the best horse I've ever worked with."

"Tell me about training her?"

"She was stubborn as they come at first. Took me three weeks just to convince her the saddle wasn't going to eat her..."

The stories carried them back to the ranch, where several trucks were parked near one of the barns. Garrett barely waited for the engine to stop before he was out and striding toward the barn doors, his long legs covering the ground quickly.

Emma followed, her ballet flats definitely not made for hurrying across the gravel, but she managed. Inside the barn, she found Garrett kneeling beside Thunder in her stall. The magnificent black horse lay on her side, heaving slightly, while Wyatt stood nearby with a worried expression.

"How long's she been down?" Garrett asked, running expert hands along Thunder's belly.

"About forty minutes," Wyatt replied. "Started showing signs of discomfort during evening feeding. Grace noticed her pawing at her bedding and called me right away."

Emma hung back, not wanting to interfere but unwilling to leave. She watched as Garrett checked Thunder's gums, felt her pulse, spoke to her in low, soothing tones that seemed to calm the distressed animal.

"Did you call Doc Sanders?"

"He's on his way," Grace confirmed from where she stood at the stall door. "Should be here any minute."

As if summoned by her words, boots sounded on the barn floor, and a tall man in his sixties appeared carrying a medical bag. "Evening, folks. Let's see what we've got here."

Emma observed as the veterinarian worked alongside Garrett, their movements efficient and practiced. They spoke in quick, technical terms about symptoms and possible treatments, while Thunder occasionally shifted restlessly.

"Classic impaction colic," Doc Sanders finally announced. "We caught it early, which is good. I'm going to give her some medication for the pain and inflammation, then we'll need to get her up and walk. Movement helps with this type."

The next hour passed in a blur of activity. Emma held leads and fetched water as needed, while Garrett and Doc Sanders worked to get Thunder on her feet. The horse's size made it a challenging task, but eventually, she stood, though shakily.

"Good girl," Garrett murmured, stroking Thunder's neck. "That's it, partner."

"Walk her for about twenty minutes," Doc Sanders instructed. "Then we'll reassess. Someone should stay with her through the night, watch for any changes, walk her for a while, then rest and repeat."

"I've got this," Garrett said immediately.

"I'll spell you at midnight," Wyatt offered, but Garrett shook his head.

"No. Come check on us in the morning, Wyatt."

Emma stepped forward. "I'll stay with you. I can help walk her, or just keep you company."

Garrett turned to her, really seeing her for the first time since they'd arrived in the barn. Her pretty dress was now dusty from the barn, and her carefully styled hair had started to come loose from its clip. But her eyes held nothing but warmth and concern.

"Emma, you don't have to-"

"I want to," she said firmly. "Besides, I've never missed a deadline in my life. I'm basically a professional at pulling all-nighters."

A ghost of a smile touched his lips. "Are you sure?"

"Absolutely sure."

Grace appeared with thermoses. "Coffee," she said as she hugged Emma. "Thank you for understanding about your date. I'm so sorry."

"Of course." Emma watched as the others began to disperse, leaving her alone with Garrett and Thunder. "So, what do we do first?"

"Walking," Garrett said, adjusting Thunder's lead rope. "Lots of walking."

They fell into a rhythm, walking slow circles in the barn's wide aisle. Thunder plodded between them, occasionally stopping to rest before Garrett urged her forward again. The barn settled into quiet, broken only by the soft sounds of horses in their stalls and their own footsteps on the packed earth floor.

"I'm sorry about dinner," Garrett said after their third circuit.

"Hey, none of that," Emma chided gently. "There will be other dinners."

He nodded, then said quietly, "When Sarah died... Thunder was the only one who saw me really break down. I'd come out here late at night, when Ellie was asleep, and just... let go. She'd stand there with her head over my shoulder, like she knew exactly what I needed."

Emma's heart ached at the image.

"Come on, girl. A few more steps," Garrett said.

They continued their slow parade, talking softly about everything and nothing. Garrett told her about Thunder's victories in cutting competitions, his voice carrying clear pride.

Grace appeared with sandwiches and more coffee around ten, then returned to the house after extracting a promise that they'd call if anything changed. The night deepened around them, stars brilliant through the barn's high windows.

Doc Sanders returned for a check around eleven, nodding with satisfaction at Thunder's improved condition. "Keep up the walking for another hour," he advised. "Then she can rest in her stall, but someone needs to check her every thirty minutes through the night."

"We've got it covered," Emma assured him.

After the vet left, they resumed their walking. Emma noticed Garrett trying to hide his yawns.

"Why don't you rest for a bit?" she suggested. "I can walk her."

"I'm fine."

"Garrett." She fixed him with a stern look. "You've been up since dawn, and you spent half the day in the saddle. Take a half an hour and rest. Thunder and I will be right here."

He hesitated, then nodded reluctantly. "Thirty minutes. Wake me if anything changes."

Emma watched as he settled onto a hay bale, leaning against a wall, his hat tipped low over his eyes. Within minutes, his breathing had deepened into sleep. She continued walking Thunder, speaking to her softly.

"You gave us quite a scare, girl. But you're going to be fine. Your human needs you."

Thunder's ears flicked toward her voice, and she nudged her shoulder gently with his nose.

"Yeah, I like him too," she confided. "Even if our first date got derailed. Though honestly?" She glanced at Garrett's sleeping form. "This might be better than an evening out on the town. Really shows a person's character, how they handle a crisis."

She let Thunder rest, then urged her forward again. "And your human? He's got character in spades."

Thunder let out a soft nicker, as if agreeing. Emma smiled, guiding her into another circuit. The barn's night sounds had become almost musical—the rustle of hay, the occasional stamp of hooves, the gentle whir of fans overhead, keeping the air moving.

Thirty minutes passed quickly. Emma approached Garrett, hating to wake him but knowing he'd want to check on Thunder. Before she could speak, his eyes opened.

"How is she?"

"Good. Walking well and she seems more comfortable."

He stood, stretching his tall frame. "Thank you." His voice carried more than simple gratitude for watching Thunder.

They settled Thunder in her stall after midnight, spreading fresh bedding and ensuring her water was clean. Garrett pulled a chair from the tack room, positioning it where he could easily see Thunder.

"You should go get some sleep," he said, though his tone suggested he didn't really expect her to leave.

"I'm staying." Emma said as she walked to the tack room and grabbed another chair. "Besides, I'm curious about something."

"What's that?"

"Earlier, you mentioned competitions. Tell me about those?"

His face lit up, and he launched into stories about Thunder's achievements in cutting competitions. Emma was fascinated, not just by the technical details of the sport, but by the way Garrett came alive talking about it.

"You really love it, don't you?" she asked during a lull.

"It's... pure," he said thoughtfully. "Just you and your horse, reading each other, anticipating moves. When it's right, it's like dancing."

"Will you show me sometime?"

"I'd like that."

Around two in the morning, Emma found herself fighting sleep.

"Here," Garrett said softly, shrugging out of his denim shirt to reveal a white t-shirt beneath. He draped the shirt around her shoulders. "You're shivering."

The warmth of the fabric enveloped her, carrying his scent—woodsy cologne, leather, and something uniquely him. "Thanks."

"Least I can do, considering this isn't exactly the evening I had planned."

"And what all did you have planned?"

"Well," he shifted in his chair, "dinner, obviously. Dancing, if you were brave enough." His voice took on a teasing note. "Though watching you with Sugar when you first got here, I had my doubts about your coordination."

"Hey!" She swatted his arm playfully. "I took ballet lessons... remember me telling you?"

"I do," His eyebrows rose. "It's hard to envision you as a ballerina."

"Those days are long behind me, that's for sure."

Their laughter mingled in the quiet space. Thunder lifted her head at the sound, nickering softly.

"Look at that..." Emma said. "We're entertaining her."

Garrett's expression softened as he looked at her. "You're something else, Emma Carlyle."

"Good something or bad something?"

"Definitely good." He reached over, tucking a strand of hair behind her ear. "Most women wouldn't stick around for this kind of first date."

"Most women haven't spent the last week falling in love with this ranch."

Their eyes met in the dim barn light, the moment heavy with unspoken meaning. Thunder chose that moment to paw at her bedding, breaking the spell.

Garrett rose to check on her, his movements swift but gentle. "She's okay, just restless."

They settled back into their chairs, closer than before. Emma found herself telling him about her decision to turn down the publishing contract she'd received early.

"You're sure that's what you want?" he asked.

"I am." She wrapped his shirt tighter around her shoulders. "These stories... they need to be told my way. No rushed deadlines, no insisted changes from an editor working with a strict publishers guidelines. Just honest stories about real people, real faith, real love."

"Like what you're living now?"

"Yes. Exactly what I'm living right now." She smiled.

When Wyatt arrived to check on them, he found them asleep in their chairs, Emma's head on Garrett's shoulder, his shirt still draped around her.

Thunder whinnied a greeting. Garrett stirred at the sound, his first instinct to check his horse. But his second was to look at Emma, still sleeping against him, her face peaceful in the early morning light.

"Good morning," he said softly when her eyes fluttered open.

"Morning." She sat up slowly, stretching. "How's our patient?"

"See for yourself."

They approached Thunder's stall together, finding her bright-eyed and eager for breakfast.

"Some night, huh?" Emma said as they watched Thunder happily munching her hay.

Garrett turned to her, his expression serious but tender. "Thank you for staying. You didn't have to."

"I wanted to." She smiled up at him. "Though I still expect that dinner and dancing someday."

"Count on it." He reached for her hand, squeezing it gently. "But Emma?"

"Hmm?"

"This?" He gestured to the barn, to Thunder, to their rumpled, dusty clothes. "This was a perfect first date."

Standing there in the early morning light, still wearing his shirt over her wrinkled sundress, Emma had to agree.

Chapter 20

Emma and Garrett stepped onto the lodge's wide front porch just as the breakfast bell rang. Despite their exhaustion from the overnight vigil with Thunder, the rich aroma of coffee and bacon drew them inside. Emma smoothed her wrinkled sundress, still wearing Garrett's denim shirt over it.

"I must look a sight," she said, running fingers through her tousled hair.

"You look fine." Garrett's quiet assurance carried a warmth that made her cheeks flush.

Before she could respond, the door burst open and Ellie bounded out, nearly colliding with them.

"Daddy! Emma! Aunt Grace said Thunder was sick, but she wouldn't let me go to the barn and—" Ellie stopped mid-sentence, her bright eyes taking in their rumpled appearance. "Why are you wearing Daddy's shirt?"

"It got chilly in the barn," Emma explained, sharing an amused glance with Garrett.

"Is Thunder better?" Ellie's concern was genuine, reminding Emma how deeply this child cared for the ranch and its animals.

"Much better, sweetheart," Garrett assured her, guiding both his daughter and Emma inside.

The dining room hummed with morning activity. Linda and Loretta moved efficiently between the kitchen and the long wooden table, laying out platters of fluffy scrambled eggs, crispy bacon, and golden biscuits. Ranch hands filled one end of the table while Tim and Carol sat near Grace, already deep in conversation about the day's planned activities.

"Well, look who finally made it to breakfast," Grace called out, her teasing tone carrying undercurrents of relief. "How's our patient?"

Garrett pulled out chairs for both Emma and Ellie before taking his own seat. "Thunder's doing well. I'm confident the colic resolved itself with treatment and walking. She's eating normally this morning."

"Thank the Lord," Loretta said, setting a fresh pot of coffee on the table. Her knowing eyes took in Emma's borrowed shirt and exhausted appearance. "Emma, honey, you look like you could use this more than anyone."

"You have no idea," Emma admitted gratefully as Loretta filled her cup.

Ellie wiggled in her seat between them. "Did you and Daddy stay up all night with Thunder? Like when I was sick with the flu and Daddy stayed up with me?"

"We did," Emma answered, reaching for a biscuit. "Sometimes the people and animals we care about need us, even if it means missing sleep."

"That's what Daddy always says." Ellie beamed at her father. "Love means being there, no matter what."

Garrett focused intently on filling his plate, but Emma caught the slight redness at the tips of his ears.

"Speaking of being there," Grace interjected smoothly, "Tim and Carol are joining us for a morning ride to Shadow Creek. Emma, you're welcome to come, though I'd understand if you'd rather catch up on sleep."

"I think sleep needs to win this round," Emma said. "Plus, I should really do some writing today after a much-needed nap."

"Are you writing about us?" Ellie asked. "About the ranch and the horses and everything?"

Emma carefully buttered her biscuit. "In a way. I'm writing stories about people who live on ranches, finding love and faith and family."

"Like you and Daddy?"

Emma felt heat rise in her cheeks as several pairs of eyes flickered their way.

"Well," Emma started carefully, "I'm writing about pretend people, but they're inspired by the wonderful people and things I've learned here at Silver Bluff."

"But you like Daddy, right?" Ellie persisted, her innocence making the question both sweeter and more pointed. "And you like it here with us?"

Emma met Garrett's gaze briefly before turning back to Ellie. "I care about everyone here very much. Your daddy, you, your aunt Grace, your grandparents—you've all made me feel so welcome."

"So you'll stay?" Hope brightened Ellie's face. "Forever and ever?"

The conversation around the table had grown quieter, though everyone pretended to be absorbed in their breakfast.

"Ellie," Garrett's voice carried a gentle warning. "Remember what we talked about? About not putting pressure on people?"

"I'm not pressuring," Ellie protested. "I'm just asking. Because Emma makes you smile more, Daddy. And she helps with the horses, and she reads me stories, and she's teaching me about writing in my journal." Her voice dropped to a whisper that everyone could still hear. "And I think she'd be a really good mommy."

Emma's heart squeezed as Garrett set down his fork, clearly struggling for words. She reached over and took Ellie's small hand in hers.

"Ellie, sweetheart, those are some of the nicest things anyone has ever said about me." She chose her words with care, wanting to be honest while protecting this precious child's heart. "I love being here with you and helping with your journal. But big decisions about staying somewhere forever—those take time and lots of thinking."

"But you're happy here, right?" Ellie's eyes searched her face. "I can tell. You smile a lot, too."

"I am very happy here," Emma agreed. "Silver Bluff is a special place, and you're a very special girl."

"More special than your books?"

A soft chuckle rippled around the table at that, breaking some of the tension.

"Different kind of special, but yes," Emma explained. "Books are wonderful, but nothing compares to real people and real love."

Loretta appeared with a fresh plate of biscuits, her timing perfect as always. "Speaking of real love, who's ready for some of Linda's honey butter?"

The conversation shifted as everyone praised Linda's legendary honey butter, but Emma noticed how Garrett's hand had found Ellie's under the table. His other hand rested near his coffee cup, inches from Emma's own, and she felt the unspoken connection between them strengthen.

"Well," Tim spoke up from down the table, "Carol and I want to thank you all for such a wonderful stay. We head home later today, but we'll definitely be back."

"You've been wonderful guests," Grace assured them. "And you're welcome anytime."

Emma used the moment to push back her chair. "It was so nice getting to know you both, Tim and Carol. If you'll excuse me, I should try to get some sleep before I fall face-first into my coffee."

"I'll walk you out," Garrett said, standing as well.

"Can I come?" Ellie asked immediately.

"No, punkin," Garrett said firmly. "Finish your breakfast. You've got riding lessons with Aunt Grace this morning."

Emma said her goodbyes, touched by the genuine warmth in everyone's responses. As she and Garrett stepped onto the porch, the morning sun had risen fully, painting the ranch in clear light.

"I'm sorry about Ellie," Garrett said. "She gets ideas in her head sometimes..."

"Don't apologize. She's processing things in her own way." Emma turned to face him. "She loves you so much, Garrett. She just wants you to be happy."

"I know." He ran a hand through his hair. "It's just... complicated."

"Life usually is." Emma smiled.

Behind them, through the open window, Ellie's voice carried clearly: "Daddy really likes Emma, doesn't he, Grandma?"

"Now, Ellie," Loretta's voice held gentle amusement, "that's not something we need to discuss at breakfast."

"But he does! I can tell. He looks at her the way Prince Charming looks at Cinderella in my book."

Emma bit her lip to keep from laughing at Garrett's mortified expression.

"Don't worry," Emma said, her eyes twinkling. "Being compared to Prince Charming isn't the worst thing."

"I wouldn't know," Garrett managed. "Fairy tales aren't exactly my area of expertise."

"No? I thought every cowboy was well-versed in happily ever after."

His expression softened, and he cleared his throat. "You should get some rest. I need to finish my breakfast and then check on Thunder."

Emma nodded, understanding his retreat.

She started down the path toward her tiny home. Behind her, she heard Ellie's voice drift through the window once more.

"Daddy? Why didn't you answer my question about Emma staying?"

"Because, sweetheart," Garrett's reply was gentle but firm, "some questions don't have simple answers."

"But if you love someone, isn't that a simple answer?"

Emma's steps slowed, her heart catching at the pure wisdom in Ellie's words. She didn't turn around, didn't want to see Garrett's expression, but she heard the emotion in his voice when he finally spoke.

"You're a smart little girl, Ellie."

Emma continued walking, feeling like an intruder on this precious moment between father and daughter. But Ellie's words followed her, stirring something deep in her soul.

Reaching her tiny home, Emma climbed the steps slowly. But instead of heading straight to bed, she opened her laptop and created a new document. The words flowed easily:

Sometimes love comes quietly, in the space between midnight conversations and morning revelations. Sometimes it comes through the honest questions of a child who sees the truth more clearly than adults ever could.

And sometimes it comes with the dawn, wrapped in a borrowed denim shirt and the courage to believe in second chances. Yet whoever knew it could come so quickly. So easily.

She saved the file, knowing these words would find their way into her story somehow. But right now, they were just for her, a testament to this moment, this place, these people who'd worked their way so deeply into her heart.

As she crawled into bed, Emma offered up a silent prayer—not for answers or certainty, but for wisdom and grace to navigate whatever lay ahead. The last thing she remembered before drifting off was the feel of Garrett's shirt around her shoulders and the echo of Ellie's simple truth: if you love someone, that's the simplest answer of all.

Chapter 21

Emma woke several hours later to the gentle patter of rain against her tiny home's metal roof. She stretched, noticing she'd fallen asleep still wearing Garrett's shirt over her sundress. The fabric carried traces of his cologne, making her smile despite her lingering tiredness.

A glance at her phone showed several missed messages, including one from Grace: "Thunder's doing great. Garrett finally got some sleep, too. Family dinner at the main house tonight—6pm. Don't you dare try to skip it!"

Emma sat up, running fingers through her tangled hair. The events of breakfast played through her mind—Ellie's earnest questions, and Garrett's careful responses. She needed to write while these feelings were fresh.

Opening her laptop, Emma began typing,

"Claire watched the rancher's daughter skip across the pasture, her small boots kicking up puffs of dust. How easily children see through adult complications, reducing years of careful walls to simple questions:

Do you love him? Will you stay? As if the answers could be as straight-forward as a summer morning..."

A knock at her door interrupted her flow. She opened it to find Ellie standing there, clutching her pink journal.

"Hi Emma! Are you still sleepy? Daddy said not to bother you, but I really need help with my story and Aunt Grace is busy with the guests and Grandma's baking and-"

"Take a breath, sweetheart," Emma laughed, stepping back to let her in.

Ellie bounced inside, claiming a spot on Emma's small couch. "I'm writing about Thunder getting sick. Because Daddy says good writers write what they know, and I know about horses getting colic."

"That's very true." Emma sat beside her, charmed by the girl's enthusiasm. "What have you written so far?"

"Well..." Ellie opened her journal, revealing random, carefully printed letters and pictures in purple ink. "I wrote about how scared everyone was, and how Daddy and you stayed up all night, like guardian angels watching over Thunder."

Emma's heart warmed at the description. "That's beautiful, Ellie. Very poetic."

"What does poetic mean?"

"It means you found a special way to say something, like comparing us to guardian angels."

Ellie beamed. "Daddy says Mommy is my guardian angel. That she watches over me from heaven." She looked up at Emma, her expression suddenly serious. "Do you think she watches over Daddy too?"

Emma took a careful breath, knowing this moment mattered deeply. "Yes, I'm sure she does, sweetheart. Moms never stop watching over the people they love."

"That's what I think, too." Ellie twisted a strand of hair around her finger. "And I think... I think maybe she helped bring you here."

"Oh?"

"Uh-huh. Because Daddy was sad for so long. He smiled and everything, but not like he really meant it. But now he smiles different." Ellie looked down at her journal, then back up at Emma. "I pray every night. I used to just pray for Daddy to be happy again. But now I pray for you too."

"You do?"

"Yep. I pray that you'll love the ranch as much as I do, and that you'll stay forever and ever, and that..." She hesitated, then rushed on, "That maybe you could love us too. Is that okay to pray for?"

Emma gathered Ellie into a tight hug, her heart full to bursting. "Oh, sweetie. It's always okay to pray for love. That's one of the most beautiful things we can pray for."

"So you're not mad?"

"Not at all." Emma pulled back to look into Ellie's earnest face. "Can I tell you a secret?"

Ellie nodded solemnly.

"I pray every night, too. I pray for guidance to make the right choices, and for wisdom to understand God's plan. And I pray for you and your daddy, that whatever happens, you'll always know how special you both are to me."

"That's a good secret," Ellie decided. She opened her journal again. "Will you help me write more about Thunder? I want to put in how you and Daddy worked together to make her better."

"Of course." Emma settled back on the couch and sent a text message to Grace so that she knew where Ellie had disappeared to. The rain continued its gentle rhythm on the roof, creating a cozy backdrop for their impromptu writing (and drawing) session.

An hour later, they had several new pages filled with Ellie's observations about Thunder's recovery, complete with child like illustrations.

"Do you think I'll be a real writer someday?" Ellie asked as she added the final touches to her drawing of Thunder.

"You already are a real writer," Emma assured her. "Anyone who puts their heart into pictures and words is a real writer."

"Like you do in your books?"

"Exactly like that."

Ellie closed her journal, hugging it to her chest. "Emma? Can I ask you something else?"

"Always."

"If... if you do stay... would it be okay if I called you Mama someday? Not right away," she added quickly. "Just... someday?"

Emma's heart squeezed painfully in her chest. She reached out and took Ellie's small hands in hers, choosing her words with the utmost care.

"Ellie, that's one of the most precious things anyone has ever asked me." She squeezed the little girl's hands gently. "But that's a very special decision that would need to involve your daddy, too."

"Because of Mommy?"

"Partly because of your mommy, yes. She'll always be your mama, sweetheart. Nothing changes that." Emma tucked a strand of hair behind Ellie's ear. "But also because these kinds of changes need to happen naturally, with lots of time and love and understanding."

Ellie considered this, her face scrunched in thought. "So it's not a no? Just a not yet?"

"It's a 'let's take things one day at a time and see what God has planned for all of us.' Can you understand that?"

"I think so." Ellie's expression brightened. "And I can keep praying about it?"

"You can always pray about anything in your heart," Emma assured her, pulling her into another hug. "That's what prayer is for."

A knock at the door made them both look up.

"Come in!" Emma called.

Garrett opened the door, his expression unreadable.

"Hi punkin'. I hope she wasn't bothering you." His eyes moved from Ellie to Emma, lingering on the denim shirt she still wore.

"Not at all," Emma said, her voice steadier than she felt. "We were having a writing session."

"Daddy!" Ellie bounced up, grabbing her journal. "Want to see what I wrote about Thunder? Emma helped me make it really good."

"I'd love to see it, but first you need to go help Grandma with the cookie dough. She's been waiting for her special helper."

"Okay!" Ellie hugged Emma quickly. "Thank you for helping with my story. And... you know... everything else."

They watched her skip down the path toward the main house, pink journal clutched tight. When she was out of earshot, Garrett turned back to Emma.

"How much did you hear before you knocked?" she asked.

"Enough. Emma, I'm sorry if Ellie put you on the spot. She gets these ideas and-"

"Stop apologizing for her beautiful heart," Emma interrupted gently. "She's processing big feelings the best way she knows how."

"She's not the only one processing big feelings." Garrett's voice dropped lower, more intimate. "I heard what you told her just now. About taking things one day at a time, seeing what God has planned."

"I meant it."

"I know you did." He moved closer, close enough that Emma could see the flecks of gold in his eyes. "That's what makes you dangerous."

"Dangerous?"

"Dangerous," Garrett repeated softly, "because you understand exactly what needs to be protected here. Ellie's heart. Our faith. The way forward." He ran a hand through his hair, a gesture Emma had come to recognize as a sign of emotional turmoil. "You fit here, Emma. In ways I never expected. In ways that terrify me."

Emma's heart thundered in her chest, but she held her ground. "Why does it terrify you?"

"Because I know what it's like to build a life with someone, to weave them into every part of your world, and then lose them. To watch your child grieve." His voice roughened. "And now Ellie's asking about calling you Mama someday, and instead of running, you gave her the perfect answer. The right answer."

"There's no perfect answer, Garrett. Just honest ones."

"See? That's exactly what I mean." He took another step closer. "You say things like that, and I just... crumble."

"Faith isn't just about enduring loss. It's also about being brave enough to embrace what God sends after the storm."

Garrett's hand moved to her face, his thumb brushing her cheek with infinite tenderness.

Emma leaned into his touch. "I've watched you with Ellie, with the ranch, with Thunder last night. Everything you do takes courage. This is just a different kind."

"Emma..." Her name was a prayer on his lips.

"Emma?--Oh!" Grace said as she stepped on the porch and peered through the screen door.

She stopped short, taking in their proximity and the charge in the air. "I'm interrupting."

"No," Garrett said quickly, stepping back. "I was just leaving." He looked at Emma, something raw and unfinished in his gaze. "Thank you for helping with Ellie's writing."

Emma watched him walk out the door, his shoulders tight with tension. Grace waited until he was out of earshot before turning to her, walking inside with raised eyebrows.

"So..." Grace held up her hands in surrender, but her eyes sparkled. "That shirt looks better on you than it ever did on him."

Emma glanced down at the denim shirt she still wore, warmth flooding her cheeks. "I should probably give it back."

"Probably," Grace agreed. "Come on. Linda made chicken and dumplings for dinner."

"Give me a few minutes for a quick shower, and then I'll come join you," Emma said with a smile.

Chapter 22

Emma curled into her favorite spot, the window seat in the tiny home. Her laptop screen illuminated the cozy space as evening settled over Silver Bluff Ranch. She could still taste Linda's delicious dinner on her lips.

Opening her blog dashboard, she began to type:

Dear readers,

Something extraordinary happens when you stop trying to write the perfect story and start living one instead.

These past few days at Silver Bluff Ranch have taught me more about authentic living, faith, and connection than all my years crafting bestselling rom-coms in Los Angeles. I've witnessed strength wrapped in gentleness, and faith tested and deepened.

The other night, I experienced my first ranch emergency. A beautiful mare named Thunder developed colic—which I've learned can be life-threatening in horses. What followed was hours of walking the barn aisles, watching skilled hands work with confidence, and seeing how a family pulls together when one of their own—even a four-legged one—needs help. (Thunder is well again, dear readers...no need to worry!)

I've learned that genuine romance isn't about perfect moments carefully crafted for social media. It's about the beautiful chaos of unplanned moments, and in dinner dates that take unexpected turns. It thrives in comfortable silences, where words become unnecessary and presence alone speaks volumes.

My past romance novels always featured grand gestures and perfectly timed declarations of love. But now I understand that love often speaks in quieter ways—like someone draping their denim shirt around your shoulders when the barn grows cold, or sharing a quiet moment with someone eating a peanut butter and jelly sandwich while sitting with a recovering horse in a barn in the middle of the night.

Love is a child's innocent prayers for happiness, or a family that welcomes you to their table as if you've always belonged there.

You all know I came to Silver Bluff Ranch seeking inspiration and knowledge for my new series of cowboy romance novels. I wanted to understand the rhythms of ranch life, to capture authentic details about horses and cattle and the Montana sky. But what I'm finding here goes so much deeper than research.

I'm discovering that faith isn't just about Sunday services and memorized bedtime prayers (though those matter too). It's about trusting enough to open your heart again after loss. It's about a little girl who sees God's hand in everything from healing horses to cookie dough. It's about understanding that sometimes the hardest parts of our journey lead us exactly where we need to be.

Remember how I told you about feeling burned out in LA? About losing my passion for writing? Here's what I didn't say then: I was afraid. Afraid of failing. Afraid of starting over. Afraid of letting go of what was familiar, even if it wasn't fulfilling anymore.

But watching this ranch family—seeing how they face each day with quiet courage and unwavering faith—it's teaching me something profound about trust. About letting go of our carefully constructed plans and allowing God to write a better story than we ever could.

This evening, I watched a grandfather sneak cookie dough when his wife wasn't looking (except she always is), and the way she pretended not to notice because sometimes love is about letting the small things slide. I witnessed a child create a cookie cutter masterpiece—a heart with a cross in the center—because in her pure wisdom; she knows that love and faith go together.

And she's right. They do.

Tonight at dinner, I watched three generations of family gather around a table laden with a simple meal of chicken and dumplings. There was more love and kindness at that dinner table than I've ever experienced at any five-star restaurant.

You see, I used to think I knew how to write love stories. I had a formula: Meet cute, conflict, resolution, happily ever after, all tied up with a perfect bow by page 312. But real love? It's messier. More beautiful. More terrifying.

It's a widowed rancher who carries grief and hope in equal measure. It's his precocious daughter who prays with complete conviction that God has good things planned for all of us. It's a family who believes in second chances, even when they're scary. Even when they require more trust than we think we possess.

My new novels aren't just going to be about cowboys and romance. They're going to be about faith that sustains through hard times. About families built not by blood alone, but by choice. About the courage it takes to open your heart when everything logical says to keep it safely guarded.

These characters growing in my mind aren't just falling in love—they're learning to trust again. They're discovering that God's plans often look different from their own, but they're always better. My characters are finding that sometimes the longest journey isn't measured in miles, but in the distance between fear and faith.

Speaking of journeys, tomorrow brings new adventures. More riding lessons (pray for my muscles, folks), more ranch work (definitely pray for my muscles), and more moments of discovery. Tonight, I'm grateful for this tiny home with its metal roof that sings in the rain, here in a small town in Montana. For a family that shares their table and their hearts. For a little girl's prayers and a rancher's quiet strength.

And I'm especially grateful for all of you coming along on this journey with me. Your messages of support mean more than you know.

With a full and happy heart,

Emma

She read through the post twice, making small adjustments before adding photos: Thunder recovering in her stall, Ellie's heart-and-cross cookie, the rainbow over Silver Bluff's pastures in between rainstorms. Her finger hovered over the image Grace had captured of her and Garrett in the barn, heads bent together as they tended to Thunder. After a moment's hesitation, she added it too.

The response was almost immediate:

"Emma, your words bring tears to my eyes. This is the most real you've ever been with us. Keep the posts coming."

"I can FEEL the love in these posts! Can't wait for the new books!"

"Oh, girl... Spill the tea, tell us more!"

"The way you write about faith and family—it's touching something deep in my soul. Thank you for sharing this journey. I think your biggest bestseller is coming soon!"

Emma smiled at the comments, then noticed a new message from her former editor at Preston House Publishing:

"Emma—Your social media engagement is through the roof. Readers are loving this authentic voice. Please call me?"

A few weeks ago, she would have jumped immediately and responded to this message. A few weeks ago, this kind of message would have felt validating. Now it didn't.

Chapter 23

Emma adjusted her grip on Sugar's reins as they rode into the north pasture, the morning air crisp against her cheeks. On either side of her, Garrett and Grace were on their own horses.

"Emma, your horsemanship improves with each passing day," Grace said.

Emma smiled as Sugar fell into perfect rhythm with the other horses.

"I couldn't have made such progress without both of you," she replied.

They crested a gentle rise, revealing a sweeping view of the pasture below. Emma caught her breath at the sight—lush grass stretching toward distant mountains dotted with grazing cattle.

"This is one of our best grazing areas," Garrett explained, pointing toward a section of fence line. "Which is why maintaining these fences is important. One weak spot, and we could lose the horses."

"And we've got a couple of spots that need attention this morning," Grace added, guiding her horse alongside Emma's. "Perfect opportunity for Fence Repair 101."

They rode toward the nearest section of fence, where several posts had begun to lean. Garrett dismounted first, his movements fluid and practiced. Emma watched, mirroring his technique as she swung down from Sugar's saddle with confidence.

"Not bad," he said, the corner of his mouth lifting. "Though you might want to bend your knees more on the landing."

"Says the man who came out of the womb riding," Emma teased, brushing dust from her jeans.

Grace laughed as she tied her horse. "Oh, he did. Mom likes to tell the story of how he tried to ride one of the sheep they used to have when he was three."

"Really?" Emma's eyes sparkled with amusement. "How did that work out?"

"About as well as you'd expect," Garrett admitted, pulling tools from his saddlebags. "The sheep wasn't impressed."

They worked their way along the fence line, Garrett demonstrating proper repair techniques while Grace added helpful tips. Emma was fascinated by the precision involved—the way Garrett tested each post's stability, how he measured the tension in the wire.

"The main thing is keeping the wire tight enough without over-stretching it," he explained, showing her how to use the fence stretcher. "Too loose, and horses can push through. Too tight, and it'll snap when the weather changes."

Emma nodded, trying to memorize every detail.

Grace handed Emma a pair of work gloves. "I saw your blog post last night. The comments were incredible."

Emma felt warmth creep into her cheeks, especially when she noticed Garrett's interest.

"I noticed you left out some of the more interesting details about that night in the barn," Grace said with a sly smile.

"Grace," Garrett warned, but his sister ignored him.

Emma focused intently on the fence post in front of her, grateful for the excuse to hide her reddening face.

"By the way, when are you two planning to attempt that dinner date again? Since Thunder so inconsiderately interrupted the first one."

Garrett paused in his work, wire tensioner in hand, and looked at Emma. "I hadn't thought about it, but..." His eyes met hers. "What about tonight?"

Emma's heart skipped at the quiet hope in his voice. "Tonight would be perfect."

"Well then," Grace said, satisfaction clear in her tone. "Now that's settled, Emma, come watch how this tensioner works. It's tricky if you don't get the angle right."

They spent the next hour working their way down the fence line. Emma discovered muscles she didn't know existed as she helped hold posts steady and learned to splice wire. But she found herself enjoying every minute, especially when Garrett's hands would cover hers to demonstrate proper technique.

"The trick is feeling the right amount of give," he explained, standing close behind her as she worked with the wire. His breath stirred her hair, and Emma forced herself to focus on the task rather than the warmth of his presence.

"Like this?" she asked, adjusting her grip.

"Perfect." His approval sent a pleasant shiver down her spine.

Grace's voice drifted from further down the line, where she was checking another post. "Emma, has anyone told you about the time Garrett got his boot stuck in a fence and had to hop home with one shoe?"

"No," Emma laughed, turning toward Grace. "When was this?"

"I was twelve," Garrett protested. "And that fence was already falling down."

"He looked like a very angry flamingo," Grace continued, ignoring her brother's objection. "Hopping across the pasture, covered in mud because it had rained the night before..."

Emma tried to suppress her giggles at the mental image. "Please tell me there are photos."

"Mom has some somewhere," Grace said. "I'll have to look through the albums."

"Don't you dare," Garrett warned, but his eyes were laughing.

"So, tell me more about what it was like for both of you growing up on this ranch. I imagine there were plenty of funny moments, but seriously... what was it like as a child?"

"Well," Grace leaned against a sturdy fence post, "it was pretty magical, honestly. Every day was an adventure."

"Except when there were chores," Garrett added, a grin playing at his lips.

"Oh, like you didn't love every minute of it," Grace countered. "Even mucking stalls."

"The horses were worth it," he conceded, checking the tension on another section of wire. "Remember that old pony, Buttercup?"

Grace burst out laughing. "The one who used to steal your hat every chance she got? How could I forget?"

Emma watched them, enchanted by this glimpse into their shared past. "What did she do with the hats?"

"Dropped them in the water trough," Garrett said, shaking his head. "Every single time. Dad finally got tired of buying new ones and made me work extra hours to pay for them myself."

"Best summer of my life," Grace sighed happily. "Watching you chase that pony around the corral..."

"You could have helped," Garrett pointed out.

"And miss the show? Never."

Emma moved to the next section of fence, getting more confident with the repair technique. "It sounds wonderful, growing up here. All this space, the freedom to explore, the animals..."

"It wasn't always easy," Garrett said, his voice softening. "Ranch life has its challenges. But there's nowhere else I'd rather raise Ellie."

"I get it," Emma admitted, looking out over the rolling pasture. The morning sun had burned away the last wisps of dawn mist, revealing the vibrant greens of the summer grass.

Grace watched Emma's face carefully. "This is all so different from what you're used to, isn't it?"

"In every possible way." Emma smiled, remembering her apartment, the constant traffic noise. "But different in the best way."

They worked steadily along the fence line. Emma finding an easy rhythm—check the post, test the wire, make repairs where needed. Her hands were getting steadier with the tools, more confident in their movements.

"You're a natural," Garrett said quietly, appearing at her side to inspect her work.

She looked up at him, caught by the warmth in his eyes.

Grace cleared her throat dramatically. "And on that note, I should head back and take care of some paperwork in the office. You two can finish up here?"

"We've got it covered," Garrett assured her.

They watched Grace mount up and ride away, her horse kicking up small puffs of dust as they trotted across the pasture.

"Your sister isn't exactly subtle," Emma said when Grace was out of earshot.

Garrett chuckled. "Never has been." He hesitated, then added, "Does it bother you?"

"Not at all," Emma said, meeting his gaze steadily. "Does it bother you?"

"No." He said, as he turned back to the fence, picking up another section of wire. "About dinner tonight..."

Emma's hands stilled on the post she was checking.

"The Silver Spur isn't exactly fine dining. Small-town Montana isn't big on fancy restaurants."

She smiled, remembering the elegant Los Angeles restaurants Liam had favored. "Good. I'd much rather have authentic than fancy. I'm not interested in being impressed. I just want to have a nice dinner with you and enjoy the atmosphere."

They worked in silence for a few minutes, moving down the fence line with efficiency. Emma watched Garrett—the way his hands moved confidently with the tools, how the morning light caught the angles of his face.

"What?" he asked, catching her looking.

"Just thinking about how different this is from my life in LA. A year ago, if someone had told me I'd be fixing fences in Montana..."

"Having second thoughts?"

"No." The certainty in her voice surprised even her. "This feels more real than anything in LA ever did. Even the hard parts."

Garrett nodded, understanding in his eyes. "Ranch life isn't always romantic. It's long hours, hard work, dealing with whatever nature throws at you."

"Like sick horses in the middle of the night?"

"Exactly." He smiled at the memory. "Though that night turned out better than expected."

Emma's heart fluttered at his words. She was about to respond when a movement caught her eye. A young foal had wandered close, curious about their activities.

"Well, hello there," she said softly.

"That's one of Misty's colts," Garrett explained. "Born about two months ago."

The colt took a few tentative steps closer, its ears perked forward with interest. Emma stayed very still, charmed by its innocent curiosity.

"Here," Garrett said, reaching into his pocket and pulling out a handful of range cubes. He placed some in Emma's palm. "Hold your hand flat."

Emma extended her hand, holding her breath as the colt approached. Its tiny tongue tickled her palm as it delicately took the treats.

"Oh!" she laughed in delight. "That's amazing."

"You're amazing," Garrett said quietly.

She looked up, startled by the tenderness in his voice. He was watching her with an expression that made her heart race.

"Most city girls wouldn't be out here learning fence repair and making friends with livestock," he continued.

"Most city girls don't have a clue what a joy this all is. They don't know what they're missing," she replied softly.

The moment stretched between them, full of unspoken possibilities. Finally, Garrett cleared his throat.

"We should finish this section before it gets too hot."

They returned to work, but something had shifted in the air between them. Their movements seemed more synchronized, their casual touches lingering just a moment longer than necessary.

The rest of the fence line repair passed quickly. As they gathered their tools and prepared to mount up, Garrett turned to Emma.

"Five o'clock?" he asked. "For dinner?"

"Five sounds perfect."

He helped her mount Sugar, his hands steady at her waist. As she settled into the saddle, he didn't immediately step back.

"Emma?"

"Yes?"

"I'm glad Thunder waylaid our plans the other night."

She looked down at him, puzzled. "You are?"

"Because now I know exactly what kind of woman you are." His eyes held hers. "The kind who stays up all night to help a sick horse. The kind who learns to fix fences and befriends and enjoys animals. The kind who makes me think that maybe..."

He trailed off, but Emma's heart filled in the rest. She reached down and squeezed his hand.

"Five o'clock," she reminded him softly.

"Five o'clock," he agreed.

They rode back toward the ranch, the morning sun warm on their backs. Emma's mind was already racing ahead to evening, but her heart was perfectly content at this moment—riding beside Garrett, the sound of hoofbeats on Montana soil, and the promise of something beautiful growing between them.

As they approached the barn, Emma noticed Ellie waiting by the corral, her pink journal clutched to her chest. The little girl's face lit up when she saw them.

"Did you fix all the fences?" she called out. "Can I help next time?"

"We did," Garrett answered, dismounting smoothly. "And maybe when you're a bit older, punkin'."

Emma let Garrett help her down from Sugar, his hands lingering at her waist.

"Did you write more stories?" Emma asked Ellie as they led the horses to the barn.

"Uh-huh! Want to read them? There's one about the kittens, and one about Thunder getting better, and one about..." Ellie glanced at her father, then back at Emma with a conspiratorial smile. "Well, maybe I'll show you that one later."

Garrett raised an eyebrow. "Should I be worried about what you two are writing?"

"Nope!" Ellie bounced on her toes. "But Grandma says a lady never reveals all her secrets at once."

Emma couldn't help laughing at Garrett's expression—a mixture of amusement and mild concern. As they settled the horses into their stalls, Ellie chattered about her morning adventures with Linda in the kitchen.

"And Grandma taught me how to make her special apple pie! She said it's a family recipe that goes back forever and ever and ever."

"Wow, sounds like you have had a busy morning, Ellie," Emma said.

"You'll have to try my pie tonight after dinner tonight," Ellie said, her voice full of innocent hope.

Emma caught Garrett's eye over Ellie's head. His smile was soft, private.

"Well, sweetheart," he said. "Emma and I have other plans for dinner. But we'll save room for dessert and have some when we get home."

"Wait!" Ellie's whole face brightened with understanding. "Are you going on a date?"

"Something like that," Garrett admitted, reaching down to ruffle his daughter's hair.

"Good," Ellie declared with satisfaction. "Because I prayed about it."

Chapter 24

Emma's heart fluttered as Garrett held open the wooden door of the Silver Spur restaurant. The chime of bells overhead announced their arrival, mixing with the warm chatter of other diners and the subtle aroma of grilled steaks and fresh-baked bread.

"Evening, Garrett!" A cheerful voice called out. The hostess, a woman in her fifties with silver-streaked dark hair, approached with menus tucked under her arm. "And this must be Emma Carlyle. I'm Connie. We've all been wondering when we'd finally get to meet you."

Emma felt her cheeks warm as Garrett's hand found the small of her back. "Word travels fast in Riverbend Valley," he explained with a quiet chuckle.

"Especially when Grace has been talking you up for days now. We're all excited about hosting such a well-known author here in our neck of the woods," Connie winked at Emma. "Come on, I've got your favorite booth ready, Garrett."

They followed Connie through the restaurant, passing tables filled with local families and couples. Emma took in the authentic Western decor—old ranch tools mounted on rough-hewn wooden walls, vintage black and white photographs of cattle drives, and iron wagon wheel chandeliers casting warm light throughout the space.

The booth Connie led them to was tucked into a cozy corner with a window overlooking Main Street and the River Walk, a scenic path alongside the Deer Run River that meandered on the edge of town. Garrett waited for Emma to slide in before taking his seat across from her.

"Your server will be right with you," Connie said, setting down their menus. "And Emma? Don't let him convince you the elk burger is better than my chicken fried steak. He's been wrong about that for years."

After Connie left, Emma opened her menu but found herself glancing at Garrett more than studying the menu. He'd traded his usual work clothes for dark jeans and a crisp blue button-down shirt that brought out the color in his eyes. When he caught her looking, his smile made her pulse skip.

"What?" he asked.

"Just thinking how happy I am that you asked me out to dinner," she admitted.

"I'm glad I did too," Garrett replied, his voice softening. "Though I should have done it much sooner."

"We had a few interruptions," Emma reminded him with a smile.

"Life on a ranch," he agreed. "Never quite goes according to plan."

Their server approached—a college-aged girl with a bright smile and a name tag reading 'Katie.' "Hi Mr. Walker! And you must be Miss Carlyle. My mom loves your books!"

Emma smiled warmly. "Thank you, that's so nice to hear."

"Can I start you folks off with some drinks?" Katie asked, pulling out her notepad.

"Sweet tea for me," Garrett said.

"Make that two," Emma added.

As Katie walked away, Emma leaned in and asked. "So, what do you recommend?"

"Well, I've never ordered anything here that I didn't like. The steaks are some of the best I've ever had."

"There is so much to choose from," Emma said, looking over the menu. "I tell you what, I'm feeling adventurous tonight. You order for me, my only request, whatever it is, the meat has to be well done."

"You trust me to order for you?"

"Absolutely."

Their easy banter continued as Katie returned with their drinks and took their orders. Emma marveled at how comfortable she felt with Garrett, how natural their conversation flowed. It was nothing like the calculated, networking-focused dates she'd experienced in LA.

"You're thinking hard about something," Garrett observed, stirring his tea.

"Just comparing this to what life is like back in Los Angeles," she admitted. "Everything there felt so... performative. Like everyone was trying to check boxes on some invisible checklist of what the perfect life should look like."

"And how does Montana measure up so far?"

"It's real," Emma said simply. "Everything here is. The people, the work, the relationships." She paused, gathering her thoughts. "When I first arrived at Silver Bluff, I thought I was just doing research for my books and taking a vacation. But being here, experiencing ranch life firsthand, getting to know people and having real and honest conversations—it's changed everything for me. The way I see the world, the way I write, what I want from life..."

Garrett's expression grew thoughtful. "And what do you want from life?"

Emma took a sip of tea, considering her answer carefully. She met his eyes. "I want to feel as alive as I do right now, forever. I'm seriously considering a few major life changes in my future."

Before Garrett could respond, Katie arrived with their appetizer—a platter of locally famous Silver Spur stuffed mushrooms. The savory aroma of herbs and melted cheese filled the air between them.

"These are incredible," Emma said after taking a bite. "I can't believe I've never had anything like this before."

"Wait until you try the main course," Garrett replied, a hint of pride in his voice. "The beef comes from our neighbor Tom Henderson's ranch."

Their conversation flowed easily as they shared the appetizer, touching on everything from Ellie's latest stories to Emma's growing confidence with Sugar. Emma was captivated by the way Garrett's eyes crinkled at the corners when he smiled, how his hands moved expressively when he talked about the ranch.

"Speaking of the ranch," Garrett said after Katie had cleared their appetizer plates, "I've been meaning to ask you something."

Emma's heart quickened. "Oh?"

"Grace mentioned your publisher reached out to you?"

Emma nodded, absently tracing a pattern on the tablecloth. "They did. They offered me a new contract."

"And how do you feel about that?"

"Honestly? A few months ago, I would have jumped at the chance. But now..." She looked up at him. "The thought of going back to writing what they want, when they want, following their formulas—it feels like putting on clothes that don't fit anymore. I declined the offer."

Their main courses arrived—perfectly grilled rib eyes for both of them, with baked potatoes, roasted vegetables, and herb butter.

"This looks amazing," Emma said, inhaling the aromatic blend of herbs and butter.

They ate in silence for a few moments before Garrett spoke again. "So, what are your plans? After your stay at Silver Bluff ends?"

The question hung in the air between them, weighted with unspoken possibilities. Emma set down her fork, meeting his gaze.

"I've been thinking about that a lot lately," she admitted. "The thing is, Garrett, I don't want to leave."

Garrett's expression shifted, a mix of surprise and something deeper flickering across his features. "You want to stay in Riverbend Valley?"

"I know it sounds crazy, right?" Emma said. "A city girl suddenly wanting to put down roots in a small Montana town. But everything has become very clear to me lately. I like it here. I'm tired of my life in LA. I don't feel like I fit in there anymore... I haven't for quite some time, in fact. I want a slower lifestyle. I want to breathe fresh air. I want to sit outside and enjoy the little things around me."

Their eyes met across the table, and Emma felt the familiar spark of connection that had been growing stronger with each passing day.

"It doesn't sound crazy at all," Garrett said, his voice low and earnest. "But what about your writing? Your career?"

"That's the beautiful part," Emma smiled, enthusiasm lighting up her face. "I can write anywhere. I can run my publishing business from anywhere as well. I can decide when and if I want to travel to market my books. As long as I have an internet connection, I'm good."

"Even from a tiny house on a ranch in Montana?" Garrett's tone was teasing, but his eyes were serious.

"Especially from a tiny house on a ranch in Montana," Emma replied. "Though I'd probably need to look for something more permanent if I do decide to take this leap."

"There are a few properties available in town," Garrett said carefully. "And the old Crawford place just west of Silver Bluff has been on the market for months."

Emma's heart skipped at the implications of his words.

"I've been praying about it," she admitted. "About what God wants for my life. And every time I think about picking up and moving, something inside me just screams... do it. Make the move. Try something new. Create a life that you want."

"I know that feeling," Garrett said. "When something feels right in your soul, like it's exactly where you're meant to be or what you're meant to do."

Their conversation was interrupted by Katie returning to check on them. After ensuring they had everything they needed, she disappeared again, leaving them in their private bubble of possibility.

"Ellie would be thrilled," Garrett said after a moment. "She's already asked me three times this week if you're going to stay forever."

Emma laughed, warmth spreading through her chest.

"This morning at breakfast, she informed me that she'd added it to her prayer list, right between asking God to help Thunder stay healthy and requesting a puppy for Christmas."

"Well, with Ellie praying for it, how could I not consider staying?" Emma's tone was light, but her eyes held Garrett's, conveying a deeper meaning.

"Emma," Garrett began, then seemed to gather his thoughts. "Having you at Silver Bluff... everything's different. Better. Do you feel this... whatever this is, that's happening between us?"

"I do."

Emma's heart thundered in her chest as he reached across the table, taking her hand in his. His callused palm was warm against her skin, grounding her in the moment.

"I've been doing some praying of my own," he continued. "About moving forward, about opening my heart again. And every time I pray about it, God keeps bringing you to mind."

Emma squeezed his hand, her throat tight with emotion. "When I came to Silver Bluff, I never expected to find a place that felt so much like home. People who feel like family. Or you."

"I've learned that God's plans are usually better than anything we could come up with ourselves," Garrett said. "Even when they come in unexpected packages."

"Like a city girl who didn't know one end of a horse from the other?" Emma teased.

"Exactly like that." Garrett's thumb traced gentle circles on her palm.

Their moment was interrupted by Katie appearing with two plates of warm huckleberry pie à la mode. "Compliments of the kitchen," she announced with a bright smile. "Connie insisted."

"Thank you," Emma said, reluctantly letting go of Garrett's hand as Katie set the desserts down.

"Just don't tell Ellie," Garrett added with a grin.

After Katie left, Emma took a bite of the pie and closed her eyes in appreciation. "This is amazing, but I have to say, I'm looking forward to trying Ellie's pie, too."

"Speaking of Ellie's pie," Garrett said, "she told me this morning that she wants to teach you her secret technique for crimping the edges. Apparently, it's vital to the recipe's success."

Emma's heart swelled at the thought. "I'd love that. She's such a special little girl, Garrett. The way she sees the world, her faith, her open heart..."

"She gets that last part from her mama," Garrett said. "Sarah never met a stranger she couldn't befriend. She would have loved you, you know."

Emma reached across the table, taking his hand again. "Tell me more about her?"

Garrett was quiet for a moment, his expression softening with memory. "She had this way of making everyone feel special. Like they were the most important person in the world when she talked to them. She loved this place—the ranch, the valley, the whole lifestyle. She used to say God painted Montana just a little brighter than everywhere else."

Garrett met Emma's eyes. "For a long time after losing her, I thought that was it. That I'd had my chance at love, and now my job was just to raise Ellie and run the ranch. But then you showed up..."

Emma's breath caught at the tenderness in his voice.

"And suddenly," he continued, "everything started feeling different. Brighter. Like God was waking something up in me that, I thought, was gone forever. And I do want to say... I sincerely appreciate your not being offended when I mention Sarah."

"Garrett," Emma whispered, her heart racing. "She is and always will be a part of you. It's important to always remember her."

"I'm not rushing anything," he assured her quickly. "I know we're both still figuring things out. But I want you to know that if you're serious about staying in Riverbend Valley... well, I'd like to be part of the reason you stay."

Emma blinked back happy tears. "You already are part of the reason I'm considering staying here," she admitted. "You and Ellie and the ranch—you're all big parts of why I can't imagine leaving."

Their eyes held across the table, the moment stretching between them full of promise and possibility. Finally, Garrett cleared his throat.

"We should probably finish this pie before the ice cream melts completely," he said, though his eyes never left hers.

Emma laughed, breaking the intensity of the moment. "Yes, we wouldn't want to waste Connie's hospitality. And I do expect a rain check on a little dancing in the future."

"Consider it done. I'll bring you back one evening, and we'll do a little two-step on the dance floor."

When they finally left the restaurant, the summer evening had painted the sky in deep purples and blues. Garrett took Emma's hand as they walked to his truck, their fingers intertwining naturally.

"I truly enjoyed myself this evening," Emma said as they reached the vehicle. "Thank you for dinner, for talking, for everything."

Garrett turned to face her, still holding her hand. "Thank you for giving this old cowboy a chance," he replied.

Chapter 25

Emma circled Sugar through the indoor arena, her confidence growing with each smooth stride. The mare responded beautifully to the lightest touch, their morning practice session flowing like a dance.

"Perfect posting trot, Emma!" Grace called from the center of the arena, where she was teaching Ellie the proper lunging technique with a gentle pony named Butterscotch. "You're doing great!"

These quiet morning practice sessions had become one of Emma's favorite parts of the day—just her, the horse, and the peaceful rhythm of hoofbeats on packed dirt.

Ellie's clear voice rang out. "Watch this, Miss Emma! I'm teaching Butterscotch to bow!"

Emma smiled as she watched the little girl demonstrate the training technique Grace had shown her.

"Remember, gentle cues," Grace reminded her niece. "Horses respond best to patience and kindness."

The morning light filtered through the arena's high windows, catching dust motes in its beams. Emma felt a deep contentment settle in her chest. This was where she belonged—not just researching ranch life, but living it. Learning it. Loving it.

"Miss Emma, do you want to practice braiding manes later?" Ellie asked, her eyes bright with hope. "I want to make Sugar and Butterscotch pretty."

"Of course, sweetheart. Maybe we can add some ribbons, too?"

Grace laughed. "My brother won't know what hit him when he sees the horses decked out in ribbons."

"There better be some blue ribbons," came Garrett's voice from the arena entrance. He leaned against the door frame, coffee mug in hand, watching them with quiet amusement.

Emma's heart did a little flip at the sight of him. Even after their wonderful dinner date two nights ago, these small moments still caught her off guard—his presence, his smile, the way his eyes seemed to find her first in any room.

"Daddy!" Ellie bounced excitedly. "Come see what I taught Butterscotch!"

Before Garrett could respond, the crunch of tires on gravel cut through the peaceful morning. A sleek black SUV pulled up outside the arena, its tinted windows and gleaming chrome jarringly out of place against the ranch's rustic backdrop.

Grace frowned. "That's odd. We don't have any new guests scheduled to arrive today."

Emma felt an inexplicable sense of dread as the back passenger's door opened. A familiar figure emerged, movie-star handsome in tailored slacks and a silk shirt that probably cost more than most people's monthly salary.

"Emma! Darling!" Liam Monarch's voice carried dramatically.

Emma's hands tightened involuntarily on Sugar's reins. The mare, sensing her tension, shifted nervously beneath her.

"Emma, who is that?" Grace asked quietly.

But before Emma could answer, Liam strode into the arena like he was walking onto a film set, his thousand-dollar shoes kicking up dust.

"Emma, sweetheart!" Liam spread his arms wide, seeming oblivious to the stunned silence that had fallen over the arena.

Emma fought to keep her voice steady. "Liam. What are you doing here?"

She saw Garrett straighten, his relaxed posture shifting to alert watchfulness. Grace moved closer to Ellie, who was staring at Liam with undisguised curiosity.

"What am I doing here?" Liam laughed, the sound practiced and perfect.

"I've had an epiphany, darling," Liam continued, moving closer to Sugar. The mare's ears flattened, picking up on the tension in the arena. "These past months without you... they've changed me. Opened my eyes."

Emma fought the urge to laugh at the rehearsed quality of his words. How many times had she heard him deliver similar lines in his movies?

"LA misses you, darling," he placed a hand over his heart, "I miss us. The power couple of page and screen. Think about it—your books, my movies, red carpets, magazine covers..."

"Liam-" Emma started, but he was too caught up in his performance to hear her.

"I've got proof that I understand your new... interests." He pulled a folded script from his jacket pocket with a flourish. "Take a look at this. It's called 'Montana Sunset.' The studio bought it just for us. You'll love it—handsome rancher, city girl writer, passionate romance under big skies…"

Grace made a small sound that might have been either a laugh or a cough. Emma noticed Garrett's jaw tightening, his hands clenched at his sides.

"Just imagine it, darling," Liam continued. "We'll shoot it right here in Montana. You can research your little cowboy stories. I'll learn to ride—well, with a stunt double for the dangerous parts, of course—and we'll show Hollywood what real ranch romance looks like!"

The absurdity of it all hit Emma like a physical force. This man, who'd never mucked a stall or fixed a fence in his life, thought he could reduce the ranch lifestyle to a glossy Hollywood production.

"Is that what you think this is?" Emma finally found her voice. "Some kind of… research project? A movie set?"

"Well, isn't it?" Liam looked genuinely confused. "I mean, surely you're not planning to stay here forever. The dirt, the animals, the…" he wrinkled his nose at the arena's earthy scents, "rustic charm. It's great for inspiration, but-"

"But what?" Emma challenged, sitting taller in her saddle. "But it's not sophisticated enough? Not glamorous enough?"

"Emma, be reasonable. You're a bestselling author. You belong in LA, at parties and premieres, not…" he gestured vaguely at the arena, "playing cowgirl."

From her position atop Sugar, Emma could see everyone's reactions. Grace's protective stance near Ellie, who was watching with wide eyes. Garrett's barely contained anger, visible in the rigid set of his shoulders. And Liam, so polished and perfect, completely blind to the real beauty and authenticity surrounding him.

"You don't get it at all, do you?" Emma said quietly. "This isn't a game or a temporary phase. These are real people, with real lives and real faith. This place..." she looked around the arena, at the morning light painting everything in honest, unfiltered clarity, "it's changed me. Really changed me, not just surface-level Hollywood changed."

"Think about everything we've built together." Liam pressed, taking a step closer to Sugar. The mare sidestepped nervously, but Emma held her steady. "Our history, our connection. Remember that night at the Golden Globes? How everyone said we were the perfect match?"

"Perfect for the cameras and the image you wanted to uphold," Emma replied. "But that's all it was, wasn't it? Just another performance."

Liam's expression shifted, a flash of calculation crossing his features before settling back into earnest charm. "You don't mean that. We had something real. I know you still love me—how could you not? We were meant for each other, darling."

"The horses need water," Garrett's deep voice cut through Liam's speech. He moved purposefully into the space between them, carrying a fresh bucket. His actions were casual, but his message was clear—this was his territory.

Liam's smile tightened almost imperceptibly. "Of course, of course. Don't let me interrupt your... chores." He managed to make the word sound slightly distasteful. "Emma, sweetheart, think about what you're doing here. Playing with horses? Living in some tiny house? This isn't you."

"Actually," Emma felt strength flowing into her voice, "this is more me than I've ever been. For the first time in my life, I'm not playing a role or trying to meet someone else's expectations."

"But your career-"

"Is transforming into something authentic," she interrupted. "Something that comes from my heart, not a publisher's marketing plan. Something that I am choosing."

"Don't throw away everything we had," Liam pleaded, his voice dropping to that intimate tone he'd perfected in countless romantic scenes. "I've changed. I see now what you need. We can make it work—you can have your little ranch adventures, and I'll support you. We'll divide our time between LA and Montana. I'll even learn to ride... eventually."

Emma watched as Garrett quietly let Butterscotch drink from the water bucket. The contrast between his natural, capable presence and Liam's artificial performance struck her forcefully.

"You know what's funny, Liam?" Emma said, gathering her reins. "Months ago, that might have sounded perfect. A compromise between two worlds. But now I realize—I don't want a compromise. I don't want to play at being authentic. I want to live it."

She slid off her horse and strode toward Liam, her voice tight with anger. "Get outside — now. You have no right barging in here, trying to take control. You're causing chaos, and there's a child present. Show some decency."

Liam followed Emma outside the arena, his perfect composure finally showing cracks of frustration. Inside, Grace distracted Ellie with grooming Butterscotch, while Garrett moved to the arena doorway, close enough to intervene if needed.

"You're making a mistake," Liam said, his voice harder now. "Look at me, Emma. Really look. I'm offering you everything you ever wanted. Fame, fortune, a platform for your writing-"

"Everything I thought I wanted," Emma corrected. "Before I learned what really matters."

"And what's that? Playing cowgirl? Living in the middle of nowhere? Writing cheap romance novels about-"

"Don't." Emma's voice cut like steel. "Don't you dare belittle this place or these people. They have more authenticity in one day than we had in our entire relationship. How dare you belittle what I do for a living... cheap romance novels... just how dare you!"

"Authenticity?" Liam scoffed. "Is that what you call this? Sweating in the dirt, sleeping in a tiny house, hanging around with..." his eyes flicked to Garrett, "local color?"

Emma felt anger rising in her chest. "Yes, that's exactly what I call it. Real people, living real lives, guided by real faith. Not just talking about values in interviews, but actually living them."

"Oh please," Liam rolled his eyes. "Since when did you become so... provincial? The Emma I know-"

"The Emma you knew doesn't exist anymore," she interrupted. "She was a character I played, trying to fit into your world. But God had different plans for me."

Liam's face twisted with disbelief. "God? Really? Now you're going to get religious on me?"

"Faith isn't a PR strategy, Liam. It's not something you put on for appearances."

"You belong in Hollywood, with me," Liam insisted, reaching for her hand. "We can have it all—the glamour, the success, and if you want... some of this rustic charm, too."

Emma pulled away from his grasp. "I don't want 'some of this.' I want all of it. The early mornings, the hard work, the simple pleasures. I want a life filled with meaning, not just appearances. I want peace and quiet. I want room to grow and learn and build the life I want for myself."

"But why?" Liam demanded. "Why choose this over everything we had?"

"Because here, I'm not just playing a part," Emma said softly. "I'm becoming who I was meant to be. Every morning when I wake up, every time I work with the horses or help with ranch chores, or write what's in my heart, I feel God's purpose for my life becoming clearer. And by the way… what we had was nothing, it was all meaningless."

Liam opened his mouth to argue further, but Garrett's steady footsteps approached from behind Emma. He moved to stand beside her, his presence solid and grounding.

Liam's expression shifted to calculated amusement. "Ah, the brooding cowboy. Classic archetype." He gave a dismissive laugh. "Let me guess—you think you understand her better than I do? That your simple, honest lifestyle has somehow transformed her?"

"No," Garrett replied calmly. "I think she transformed herself."

"How quaint," Liam sneered. "The noble rancher defending his lady's honor. Tell me, what can you possibly offer her? A life of manual labor? Endless chores? Living in the middle of nowhere, cut off from everything that matters?"

Emma watched Garrett's hands clench into fists, saw the muscle working in his jaw. But when he spoke, his voice remained steady.

"Everything that matters?" Garrett echoed. "Like what? Red carpets and fancy parties? Empty promises and shallow relationships?"

"You know nothing about our world," Liam shot back.

He turned to Emma then, his eyes softening as they met hers. "This isn't my fight. You're the one who needs to tell him to leave if you want him to. I'm here if you need me."

Emma felt strength flowing through her, born of certainty and faith.

"I loved the idea of us, Liam," she said. "The fairy tale version of love that looked perfect on magazine covers. But it was never real. It was all surface, no substance."

"Emma, don't-"

"I've found something real here," she continued, her voice growing stronger. "Something true and deep and meaningful. Something you'll never understand because you're too caught up in appearances to see what really matters."

"You can't be serious," Liam scoffed. "You're choosing this... this cowboy and his dusty ranch over everything we could have?"

"No," Emma said firmly. "I'm choosing myself. The person God created me to be, not the persona you wanted me to maintain. I'm choosing faith over fame, substance over style, and love over appearances."

She felt Garrett's hand brush against hers, a subtle gesture of support that sent warmth spreading through her chest.

"Go back to Hollywood, Liam."

Liam's carefully maintained facade cracked, revealing the anger beneath. "You're making the biggest mistake of your life," he spat, his movie star charm evaporating. "When this little ranch fantasy of yours falls apart, don't come crawling back to me."

"The only fantasy," Emma replied calmly, "was thinking Hollywood's version of happiness was enough."

"You think this is real?" Liam gestured wildly at the surrounding ranch. "Playing pioneer woman with your cowboy? Writing cheap stories about-"

"That's enough," Garrett's voice carried the quiet authority of a man used to being heard. "You've said your piece. Now leave."

Liam's face twisted with contempt. "Or what? You'll challenge me to a duel at sunrise?" He laughed bitterly. "This isn't one of her romance novels."

"No," Emma said. "It's better. Because it's real." She squeezed Garrett's hand. "And you're right about one thing—this isn't a novel. In my books, the arrogant ex usually has a redemption arc. But in real life, sometimes people just need to exit stage left."

Liam's jaw clenched. He straightened and brushed off his pants, trying to reclaim his dignity. "Well, I suppose this little performance has made your choice clear. Enjoy your... rustic adventure." He turned on his heel, stalking back to his SUV. "Don't say I didn't try to save you from this... provincial existence."

"Goodbye, Liam," Emma called after him. "I'll pray for you."

He paused at his car door, throwing her one last wounded look. "Really, Emma? Prayer? You've gone completely native."

As the SUV's engine roared to life, kicking up dust in its hasty departure, Emma felt the tension drain from her shoulders. She turned to find Grace and Ellie watching from the arena doorway.

"Are you okay?" Grace asked.

Emma looked around at their concerned faces—Grace's supportive smile, Ellie's worried eyes, and Garrett's steady presence beside her. A wave of gratitude washed over her.

"I'm better than okay," she said.

"That man wasn't very nice," Ellie declared. "He talked like he was in a movie."

Grace laughed. "Out of the mouths of babes."

"He was in movies, actually," Emma explained, smoothing Ellie's hair. "But you're right—he wasn't being very nice."

"Speaking of real," Grace said, "I believe we have horses waiting to be groomed and ribbons to braid. Unless you'd rather take some time to-"

"No," Emma interrupted firmly. "I want to get back to normal. Back to what matters."

Chapter 26

Emma urged Sugar forward along the trail, her thoughts unsettled. Wilderness and wildflowers surrounded her, but even Montana's pristine landscape couldn't quiet the echo of Liam's words in her mind.

"Provincial existence," she muttered, adjusting her grip on the reins as Sugar navigated a rocky patch. "As if he has any idea what real living looks like."

A meadowlark's song pierced the morning quiet, momentarily drawing Emma from her brooding. She watched the bird take flight, envying its certainty of direction.

Sugar's ears pricked forward as they rounded the bend, the old homestead coming into view. Emma's chest tightened at the sight of the weathered logs, remembering how alive with possibility everything had felt when Garrett first brought her here.

Emma guided Sugar to the hitching post, her movements automatic after weeks of practice. The mare stood quietly as Emma secured the reins and retrieved her notebook from the saddlebag.

The homestead's porch greeted her with creaks as she settled against the rough-hewn logs. Emma pulled her knees up, balancing her notebook against them.

"What am I doing?" she whispered to the empty landscape.

Every dream she'd built over the past weeks felt suddenly fragile. Moving to Montana, leaving behind her established life in LA, switching to self-publishing her books—seen through Liam's lens. It all seemed impulsive, even reckless.

Emma opened her notebook, touching the fresh page with hesitant fingers. She'd always found clarity through writing, even if the words were just for herself.

"Okay, Emma," she murmured. "Time for some honest conversation with yourself."

Her pen moved across the page.

Reasons to Stay in LA:
Established career/publisher connections
Parents nearby
Familiar surroundings
Easy access to everything

She stared at the list, realizing how hollow each point felt. Her "established career" had left her creatively drained. Her parents, while loving, were so embedded in Hollywood's artificial world that real conversations had become nearly impossible. And "easy access to everything"—when was the last time she'd actually enjoyed LA's endless amenities?

She started a new list:

Reasons to Move to Montana:

Creative freedom
Authentic community and people
Connection to nature, wild and free
Space to breathe and think
Chance to build something real for myself

Emma lowered her pen, watching a pair of hawks circle overhead. Their wings caught invisible currents, moving in perfect synchronization. Something about their effortless dance spoke to her soul.

"Remember when you first arrived here?" she asked herself softly. "How terrified you were of everything—the horses, the work... questioning if you had gone crazy by dropping everything and reserving a tiny home on a dude ranch?"

Now she couldn't imagine starting her day without the rhythm of ranch life. The morning greetings from Linda in the kitchen. Grace's patient instruction. Ellie's infectious enthusiasm. Garrett's...

Emma closed her eyes. Garrett. The way he saw straight through to her soul. Saw who she really was. How he challenged her, supported her, believed in her capacity to learn and grow.

She turned to a fresh page.

Who I Was in LA:
Always "on"
Constantly networking
Writing what others wanted
Living up to expectations
Afraid to take risks

The truth of those words stung. She'd spent years shaping herself to fit into other people's visions—publishers, agents, Liam, even her parents. Always calculating the angles, managing her image, playing it safe.

Who I Am in Montana:
Present in the moment
Connected to something larger
Writing from my heart
Living authentically
Happy
Smiling more, worrying less
Brave enough to fail

Emma traced her fingers over the words. This was the core truth Liam couldn't grasp—she wasn't playing at being someone new. She was finally becoming who she'd always been meant to be.

A gentle breeze stirred the wildflowers, carrying their sweet fragrance to the porch. Emma breathed deeply, remembering her first sight of these mountains. How impossibly far from her comfort zone they'd seemed. Now they felt like home.

"Lord," she prayed quietly, "I know You led me here for a reason. Help me trust that path, even when doubt creeps in."

She looked down at her notebook again, seeing her lists with fresh eyes. The LA advantages were all external things—career connections, convenient amenities, familiar routines. But Montana offered something deeper—a chance to live with purpose.

"It's not about choosing between city and country," Emma realized. "It's about choosing between the person I pretended to be because it was what I knew and what I was used to and the person You created me to be."

Sugar nickered, drawing Emma's attention to the trail. Her heart skipped as she spotted a familiar figure on horseback approaching in the distance. Even at this range, she'd know Garrett's straight-backed posture anywhere.

Emma smiled, feeling the last threads of doubt dissolve. She didn't need Hollywood's version of a perfect life. She needed this—mountains and meadows, honest work and real relationships. A place where faith wasn't a carefully curated image but a living, breathing part of daily life.

She watched Garrett's steady approach, anticipation building in her chest.

The future stretched before her like Montana's endless sky—wide open with possibility.

Chapter 27

Emma watched Garrett secure his horse beside Sugar. Her heart quickened, the way it always did in his presence, even as her mind still processed the morning's confrontation with Liam.

Garrett paused at the bottom of the worn wooden steps. "Mind if I join you, or do you need more time alone?"

Emma tucked her notebook aside. "Please stay. I could use the company."

He settled beside her, close enough that their shoulders almost touched.

"Want to talk about what happened earlier?" Garrett asked.

Emma drew her knees up, wrapping her arms around them. "I keep thinking about how different everything looks now. When Liam showed up, spouting all that nonsense about Hollywood and fame... it was like watching a movie I could have been in, but I don't recognize that character anymore."

"And how do you feel about that?"

"Truthfully?" Emma turned to meet his steady gaze. "I feel relieved. Seeing him there, so artificial and calculated... it confirmed everything I've been feeling since I came here. The life I was living before—the endless networking, the shallow relationships, writing about what other people wanted instead of what was in my heart—it wasn't just unfulfilling. It was suffocating me."

Garrett nodded thoughtfully. "Sometimes we don't realize how heavy a burden is until we set it down."

"These past weeks at Silver Bluff... I've discovered who I really am. Not just as a writer, but as a person. Here, I can breathe. Think clearly. Listen for God's guidance instead of just chasing the next trend or contract."

"And what's that guidance telling you?"

Emma touched the notebook beside her. "That I want to stay in Montana. Not just at the ranch—though I'd love to keep visiting if that's okay after... well, after Liam's dramatic performance." She glanced at him uncertainly.

"Emma." Garrett's voice held a note of gentle rebuke. "Nothing that happened this morning changed how any of us feel about you being here. If anything, seeing how you handled yourself... it just confirmed what we already knew."

"Which is?"

"That you belong here. Maybe not exactly here at Silver Bluff, but in this life. This community."

Warmth spread through Emma's chest at his words. "I've been looking at some properties in Riverbend Valley. Small places with enough land for a garden, maybe a couple of horses, eventually. Somewhere I could write and build a life that feels good."

"You've given this some thought," Garrett observed.

"I have. But I also don't want to rush into anything. My apartment lease in LA runs for another four months, and I should probably take time to really plan things out."

Garrett shifted slightly, his arm brushing against hers. "You know, if you wanted more time to figure things out, one of the tiny homes could be yours for as long as you like. Give you space to write, think things through."

"Really?" Emma turned to him, hope brightening her features. "You wouldn't mind?"

"Mind?" Garrett's lips curved into a smile. "Having you around a while longer? Can't say that would be a hardship."

Emma laughed softly, then grew serious. "It's strange, isn't it? How quickly everything has changed? Not long ago, I was just another guest booking a stay at a dude ranch. Now..."

"Now?"

"Now I can't imagine my life without this place. Without Grace's friendship and Ellie's joy and..." she hesitated, then finished softly, "without you."

Garrett reached for her hand, his callused fingers intertwining with hers. "I know what you mean. When Grace first told me she'd rented the tiny house to a romance writer from LA, I thought she'd lost her mind."

"And now?"

"Now I'm thanking God." He squeezed her hand gently. "Emma, I haven't felt this way since... well, for a long time. And I'll admit, it scared me at first. But watching you with Ellie, seeing how naturally you fit into ranch life, into my life, even the way you handled Liam today... I know this isn't just some passing attraction."

"It's not," Emma agreed. "What I feel for you... it's deeper than anything I've experienced before. This is real. Sometimes overwhelmingly real."

"Too overwhelming?"

"No." Emma's response was immediate. "That's what amazes me. Despite how quickly it's happened, despite all the changes and challenges... being with you feels right. Like coming home to a place I didn't even know I was looking for."

Garrett was quiet for a moment, his thumb tracing circles on her palm. "You know, when Sarah died, I thought that was it for me. Thought God had given me one great love."

Emma waited, giving him space to continue.

"But lately, I've been thinking about something Pastor Sam said at church last month. About how God's plans for us are bigger than our own limited vision. How sometimes what we think is an ending is really just preparation for a new beginning."

"Do you believe that?" Emma asked.

"I do." Garrett turned to face her fully. "Emma, I don't know exactly what the future holds. But I know I want to find out with you beside me."

Tears pricked at Emma's eyes. "I want that too."

They sat in silence for a moment, listening to the horses shift and snort at the hitching post. A meadowlark trilled nearby, its song carrying across the peaceful landscape.

Finally, Garrett stood, offering Emma his hand. "Dance with me?"

Emma blinked in surprise. "Here? Now?"

"Can't think of a better place or time."

She placed her hand in his, letting him pull her to her feet. "Always, cowboy."

Garrett drew her close, one hand settling on her waist while the other kept hold of hers. They began to sway together on the old porch, its boards creaking a rustic accompaniment to their movement.

"You know," Emma said, resting her head against his chest, "when I came here to research ranch life, I never expected to find this kind of romance."

"Better than your books?"

"So much better." She lifted her face to his. "Never stop romancing me like this, Garrett."

His eyes softened as he gazed down at her. "Never."

When his lips met hers, Emma felt the rightness of it all the way to her soul. This wasn't a scene from one of her novels or a moment staged for cameras. This was real love, built on faith and understanding, growing stronger with each passing day.

Behind them, the horses nickered softly, as if offering their approval. The Montana wind whispered through the grass, carrying the scent of sage and wildflowers. And on the weathered porch of an old homestead, two hearts beat in perfect rhythm, dancing to a song only they could hear.

Epilogue

Emma's fingers flew across her laptop keyboard, putting the finishing touches on her latest blog post about ranch life and self-publishing. The autumn breeze rustled through her tiny home's open windows, carrying the familiar scents of hay and horses.

Her phone buzzed on the desk. Emma glanced at the screen, expecting another message from her growing community of self-published author friends. Instead, she saw Grace's name and two simple lines that made her heart leap:

"Come quick! It's here!"

Emma bolted upright, her chair scraping against the floor. "Oh my goodness, oh my goodness!" She barely remembered to grab her jacket as she flew out the door, boots pounding against the wooden steps.

The distance between her tiny home and the main lodge had never felt so long. Emma's heart raced as she sprinted to the lodge, hardly noticing the curious glances from the dude ranch guests.

She burst through the lodge's back door, slightly winded, and skidded to a stop. The scene before her made her heart swell. Everyone she loved was gathered around the long dining room table, their faces bright with anticipation. In the center sat a large cardboard box that made Emma's hands tremble.

"They're really here?" Her voice quavered as she pressed her hands against her mouth.

Ellie bounced on her toes, her braids swinging. "Miss Emma! Miss Emma! Can we open it now? Please?"

Garrett stood beside the box, his smile warm and knowing. His hand rested on the cardboard like he was guarding a treasure. "Well, darlin'? Would you like me to do the honors?"

Emma could only nod, too overwhelmed to speak. She watched as Garrett pulled out his worn pocket knife, carefully slicing through the packing tape. The room fell silent except for the soft crinkle of cardboard as he folded back the flaps.

Garrett reached inside and slowly withdrew a book. Emma's book. The cover caught the light, making the embossed title shimmer: "Montana Sunsets."

"Oh," Emma breathed, stepping forward. Her fingers trembled as she took the book from Garrett's hands. The weight of it, solid and real, brought tears to her eyes. "I really did it."

"You sure did, honey," Grace said, wrapping an arm around Emma's shoulders. "And it's stunning."

Linda wiped her eyes with her apron. "Our girl's a published author!"

"Self-published," Judd corrected proudly, his arm around Loretta. "Did it her own way, just like she said she would."

Emma ran her fingers over the cover, tracing the letters of her name. The story inside—her story of faith, love, and finding home on a Montana ranch—represented everything she'd discovered about herself over the past months.

"Read us something!" Ellie pleaded, pressing against Emma's side.

Emma opened to the dedication page, her voice soft with emotion as she read:

"To the family God led me to at Silver Bluff Ranch—thank you for showing me what real love looks like, in all its wonderful forms. And to everyone searching for their true path—trust His plan. Sometimes the longest way around turns out to be the shortest way home."

"That's really nice, Emma," Loretta sniffed, dabbing at her eyes with a handkerchief.

Ellie suddenly grew very still, which immediately caught Emma's attention. The little girl's usual boundless energy had transformed into an almost solemn demeanor.

"Miss Emma?" Ellie's voice was serious as she moved to stand directly in front of her. "I have something super important to ask you."

Emma knelt down, bringing herself eye-level with the child who'd stolen her heart months ago. "What is it, sweetie?"

The room grew incredibly quiet. Emma noticed Grace pressing her hands together, tears already forming in her eyes. Then movement caught her attention as Garrett stepped forward, lowering himself to one knee beside his daughter.

Emma's heart stopped as Ellie reached into her pocket and pulled out a sparkling diamond ring.

"Will you marry us?" Ellie asked, her eyes bright with hope and love.

The book slipped from Emma's hands as both palms flew to cover her mouth. Tears spilled down her cheeks as she looked between Ellie's hopeful face and Garrett's tender expression.

"Emma," Garrett's voice was rich with emotion, "these past months, you've brought so much joy and light back into my life. You've shown me that God's love is bigger than our past hurts, that He can restore what we think is lost forever. Would you do me the honor of becoming my wife and Ellie's mama?"

"Yes," Emma managed through her tears, "Yes, absolutely yes!"

Ellie squealed and launched herself into Emma's arms, and Garrett took the ring from his daughter's small fingers. His hands were steady as he slipped the diamond onto Emma's trembling finger.

"It's perfect," Emma whispered, admiring how the stone caught the light. "Just like this moment."

The room erupted in celebration. Grace rushed forward to hug them all, creating a tight family knot of joy and tears. Linda disappeared into the kitchen and returned moments later with a bottle of sparkling cider and her famous snickerdoodle cookies, this time decorated with tiny wedding bells.

"I knew it!" Linda declared, passing out glasses. "The minute you walked into my kitchen that first morning, determined to learn ranch life, I just knew you belonged here."

"We all did," Grace agreed, raising her glass. "To Emma—the newest official member of the Walker family!"

"To Emma!" everyone echoed.

Garrett pulled Emma close, pressing a kiss to her temple. "You've made me the happiest man in Montana, darlin'."

"And me, the happiest girl!" Ellie added, still clinging to Emma's waist. "Can I call you Mama now?"

Fresh tears spilled down Emma's cheeks as she knelt to hug Ellie properly. "Nothing would make me prouder, sweet girl."

Loretta cleared her throat. "Well now, we've got ourselves a wedding to plan! And don't you worry about a thing, honey. We'll help you create the perfect ranch wedding."

"Speaking of perfect," Grace interjected, "you do realize what today is, don't you?"

Emma smiled. "Exactly four months since I first arrived at Silver Bluff."

"Four months since God led you right where you needed to be," Garrett said.

"And where I'll stay forever," Emma promised, squeezing his hand.

The celebration continued through the afternoon, with ranch guests stopping by to offer congratulations and admire both the engagement ring and Emma's newly published novel. Emma found herself constantly touching the ring, hardly able to believe this wasn't one of her romance novels but her real life.

As the sun began to set, Garrett suggested they take a ride up to their special spot—the old homestead where they'd shared their first dance. Emma readily agreed, and soon they were mounting up, Emma on Sugar and Garrett on his stallion.

"Can I come too?" Ellie asked, already reaching for her riding helmet.

"Not this time, princess," Garrett said gently. "But how about tomorrow? We all ride up together and have a picnic? We can start planning the wedding."

Ellie considered this, then nodded. "Okay. But can we have chocolate chip cookies at the picnic?"

"I think that can be arranged," Emma said.

Grace stepped forward to take Ellie's hand. "Come on, sweetie. Let's go inside and find something fun to do."

As they rode toward the homestead, Emma's heart felt fuller than she'd ever thought possible. The engagement ring caught the fading light, sending tiny sparkles dancing across Sugar's mane.

"Penny for your thoughts?" Garrett asked as they approached the familiar clearing.

"I was just thinking about everything that's happened these past few months," Emma replied. "How amazing every experience has been. How everything has just seemed to have fallen into place amazingly."

Garrett smiled and nodded.

"God's plans are so much bigger than our own," Emma mused. "When I first came here, I thought I was just doing research for a book and vacationing. Instead, I found my whole life."

"And I found mine."

Emma glanced at Garrett as their horses ambled along the trail. "I have an idea."

"Tell me," Garrett said, his eyes brightening. "Another idea for your next book?"

"No," she replied, a smile playing at her lips. "This is much better."

The homestead emerged through the trees, and Emma urged Sugar into a trot, guiding her mount to the center of the meadow where she stopped. Garrett followed, bringing Thunder alongside her horse.

With her heart racing, Emma turned to Garrett and extended her hand. As his warm fingers entwined with hers, she said, "I want to be married right here."

"I agree," he murmured, leaning toward her. Emma met him halfway, their kiss sealing their promise beneath the open sky.

Leave A Review

If you enjoyed this book, please consider leaving an honest review on Amazon or Goodreads.

Visit Our Website:
www.tarabaisden.com
Visit Our Amazon Author Page HERE

Find Us On Social Media:
Facebook
Facebook Author Page
Instagram
TikTok
Threads
BlueSky

www.ingramcontent.com/pod-product-compliance
Lightning Source LLC
Chambersburg PA
CBHW010611310726
48969CB00010B/2647